About th

Dr Jayne Seagrave is a bestselling writer of guidebooks on women's travel and camping, a successful international entrepreneur and an extensively published academic. She is the author of *Camping BC, The Rockies and Yukon* (now in its ninth edition), wrote the first introductory textbook on policing in Canada and has also published books on marketing new inventions and a Canadian Shakespearean Theatre Company. *The Games Women Use* is her first work of fiction. Her infectious energy, joie de vivre and desire to convey her knowledge, experience and interests to others have resulted in an eclectic career. Born in England, Jayne moved to Vancouver in 1991 to complete her PhD in criminology. After initially working in academia, she radically changed career path and, along with her inventor husband, Andrew, established *The Vancouver Tool Corporation* (www.vancouvertool.com). She has two adult sons, Jack and Sam, adores travelling, the outdoors, and spending time with her girlfriends. Learn more at jayneseagrave.com.

THE GAMES WOMEN USE

JAYNE SEAGRAVE

THE GAMES WOMEN USE

Vanguard Press

VANGUARD PAPERBACK

© Copyright 2021
Jayne Seagrave

The right of Jayne Seagrave to be identified as author of
this work has been asserted by her in accordance with the
Copyright, Designs and Patents Act 1988.

A CIP catalogue record for this title is
available from the British Library.

ISBN 978 1 80016 153 5

Vanguard Press is an imprint of
Pegasus Elliot MacKenzie Publishers Ltd.
www.pegasuspublishers.com

First Published in 2021

Vanguard Press
Sheraton House Castle Park
Cambridge England

Printed & Bound in Great Britain

For Jacqui, Julie and Janine

Acknowledgements

In 2010 Vancouver hosted the Winter Olympics. At that time, I had the idea to step away from non-fiction and write a novel set against the background of the Olympic Games. My children were young, and I was working full time, so the idea languished, but for the next decade, whenever there was an Olympic Games, I thought of my ambition for the story existing only in my head. In 2019 I spoke to my son, Jack, who told me he was bored of hearing me talk about this unfulfilled desire and just 'get it done'. It became my 2020 New Year's resolution. In January 2020 I went to the Caribbean island of Martinique, alone, for three weeks, with an ambition to work on the novel. After six days on the island, I suffered a seizure and spent the next ten days in hospital. I remember little. Upon returning to Canada, and as therapy, I started to write *The Games Women Use*. The 2020 Tokyo Olympics were then delayed until July 2021.

This is my first work of fiction, and therefore is in stark contrast to anything else I have previously published. For as long as I can remember, my girlfriends have been pestering me to write a novel, all of them believing there is little merit saying you have a friend who has published a book on the police, or camping, or business. In contrast, there is appeal if you can boast of a friend who has written a novel, with even greater kudos if that work features women and their relationships with one another, and their partners. My first debt of gratitude must therefore be to my girl friends (and some male friends) for their support, encouragement, and strong friendships over the years. These friendships, of course, informed the narrative.

My two sons, Jack Seaberry and Sam Seaberry and their father, Andrew Dewberry remind me constantly there are absolutely no economic reasons why anyone would write a book, while at the same time offering space and time for me to pursue the lonely pursuit of crafting over 60,000 words. My family continue to provide stability, and grounding to my eclectic, ever changing, literary and personal ambitions.

Finally, the wonderful staff at Pegasus Publishing offered encouragement from the outset for me to write in another genre, provided support, sage advice and editorial guidance, resulting in the creation of a book I believe we can all be proud of.

Jayne Seagrave
Summer 2021

Contents

Chapter 1
What Happens in Vegas…
Las Vegas, May 2009

Jo Weatherspoon glanced away from her novel upon feeling the plane descend. The sky was clear, and she could see the desert below. No roads, no vegetation; just diverse colours of rock glistening in the shimmering heat haze. This was her tenth descent into Las Vegas over the course of the last eight years, and it always surprised her that, unlike so many other North American towns, Vegas did not sprawl. Vegas defied all rules of physical geography having been placed in the middle of nowhere. One moment flying over barren earth; the next encountering neon lights. True, there was a large urban area surrounding The Strip, which housed the workers whose livelihoods depended on the gamblers, call girls and tourists, but that ended abruptly when the orange rock took over. Jo rested her forehead on the window, feeling the soft vibration of the plane's engines, and stared through the thick glass as the words she could recount by heart cut into her thoughts. 'The captain has turned on the seatbelt signs as we are starting our final descent into Las Vegas.'

Glancing down at her closed novel, she started to peel the promotional '20% Off' sticker from the cover. She never read on the final approach. Despite flying at least twenty times a year, often to places visited on numerous prior occasions, landings were always the most exciting part of the journey. They confirmed arrival to a different location which, even if only a few hundred miles from home, inevitably had a different smell, temperature and feel. Flying was never boring; always stimulating. It awarded a unique way to see the environment about to be visited; a vision frequently denied to the many living there. She remembered how annoyed she was with David, when they had flown into Sydney for the first time, as he did not share this wonderment. While she strained to see the Sydney Opera House, Harbour Bridge and the miles of beaches featured in every Australian tourist brochure they had pored over when planning their sojourn, he stayed glued to his film, completely uninterested in the city where they had chosen to spend their honeymoon. Was this the first inkling she had, twenty years ago, that their relationship was not perfect? At that time there were so many dreams of a shared life together, careers, families, children… Better not go there now, she thought, as her eyes brimmed with tears and she strained to recognise the sphinx and pyramid of Luxor Palace, realising how close they were to the airport. Better, instead, to focus upon the four days at hand: the National Hardware Show and her company's investment — at her insistence

— of the forty-foot by ten-foot booth at a cost of over forty-thousand dollars, and the anticipated sales leads this investment should generate. This was a major event for the do-it-yourself (DIY) building-supply industry, and one requiring close monitoring. But this occasion was also to be followed by four days with her best friends, Kate, Daphne and Andrea, in celebration of their fiftieth birthdays. Jo smiled to herself in anticipation of the week ahead of her, as the plane — buffered by the cross winds — landed at one of the few airports in the Western world still smelling of cigarette smoke.

Jo

Jo, Kate, Daphne and Andrea met in 1984 at the University of British Columbia (UBC) in Vancouver, Canada and like many friendships forged in an academic setting, became lifelong friends. Their stable relationship confirmed by letters, cards, emails, texts and telephone calls had been well maintained over the years, with somewhat irregular get-togethers alternating between North America and Europe. These meetings were in no small part dependent upon where the burgeoning home improvement industry was holding a trade show or convention, as Jo was the international sales director for Holden Sealants, a large sealant manufacturer. When Jo attended these events, she often invited her friends to join her.

Most of the bathrooms in Europe — and to an increasing extent, North America and Japan — utilised Jo Weatherspoon's employer's sealant. Since starting work in 1985, in London, as one of over two hundred sales representatives employed across the globe, she had — to no small extent — been responsible for her firm now being internationally recognised as one of the largest and most successful sealant companies in the world. Her employers acknowledged this honour a year ago by making her Director of International Sales.

For the last five years, Jo's role involved a considerable amount of international travel, and there were advantages. The elite hotels and suites Jo commanded, while travelling on business, provided the venues for the university friends' get-togethers, to reaffirm their ties and catch-up on what the previous years had delivered to them all. In 2009, the year they all turned fifty, this venue was the Hilton Hotel in Las Vegas.

While many encountering her for the first time would have thought her executive persona and confidence was innate, this was not the case. Twenty-five years earlier, Jo arrived in Canada from England, on a Rotary Club Scholarship, to take a Master of Business Administration (MBA) at the prestigious Sauder School of Business at the University of British Columbia in Vancouver. Extremely nervous, knowing no one, she met the other women on the first day of classes, 7th September 1984. Despite their divergent degrees, all were required to take a postgraduate 'Introduction to Statistics' course. Kate, the most confident, was taking her part-time master's degree in Criminology, and was a police officer in the Royal Canadian Mounted Police in Vancouver. Andrea, a nurse, had a leave of absence to obtain her advanced diploma in paediatrics. Daphne's first degree was English Literature, and she was now embarking on a law degree. They were immediately grouped together and told to work on a range of forthcoming assignments. Unlike most professor-initiated groupings, this one worked, in no small way because of their divergent academic interests, intelligence, sense of humour and age, but mostly because it was the time of their lives when they all sought secure, supportive, unthreatening female friends; something missing prior to this time.

After introducing themselves and making quips over being thrown in at the deep end, Kate demonstrated her leadership and organisational abilities by suggesting they adjourn for coffee, to get to know each other better, and formulate a plan over who would undertake which aspects of the assigned workload. Jo knew of 'The Bean' café, walking past it regularly from her university rooms, and suggested they go there. While somewhat strained at first, once the caffeine kicked in and the conversation began to flow, they soon found they were sharing background information and arranging to meet the next day. The following weeks saw their relationship grow and within four months, Daphne suggested they leave their respective households and move in together, in a house she had found a couple of miles from the university. For the next eighteen months, until Jo returned to England, they saw each other every day, cementing the bond which would go on to last a lifetime.

In these early days at the University of British Columbia, it was Jo who was the most lost and dependent on her new friends. She arrived in North America, for the first time, just four days before classes started, to a small university-assigned, prison-like accommodation cell. Despite these anomic surroundings, she immediately fell in love with her new environment, never having breathed such fresh air, seen bald eagles flying overhead nor encountered such polite people. For the first time in her life, her northern English accent, which gave away her background and income status in England, was not a disadvantage. She marvelled at the way she could not assign Vancouverites a social class; a trait both refreshing and unnerving.

This was Jo's big escape. It was in Canada that she gained confidence and an energy suppressed in England. Over the course of her 23 years, she had been remarkably unexceptional, a characteristic she was ready to acknowledge, if only to herself. Academically she succeeded, and teachers and colleagues praised her diligence and hard work, but she was anything but exciting. Always interested in sports, she found she was often happiest by herself, working out in the gym or going for a run, than being with others. For a brief period during her undergraduate studies, she did take part in a women's rugby team, enjoying this sport, but stopped following an injury, when none of her team members noticed her absence, nor tried to contact her to ask after her wellbeing.

While contemporaries boasted at least one embarrassing incident in their teenage years to recount, she had none. There was not an inappropriate tattoo; she had not lost her virginity behind the scout hut when fifteen, nor ever drunk an excessive amount of alcohol. Having left home at eighteen to attend university, the only child of a stay-at-home mother and plumber, who was now retired, her life prior to UBC had been predictable, conservative and safe. Her parents were in their forties when she was born and although loving them dearly, she was aware that part of her social ineptness was the result of this parentage; the fact she was an only child of provincial working-class northerners.

Certain people grow into their bodies and their looks as they age, and Jo was one of these. She was not stunningly attractive but as she matured, spent more time on physical fitness and lost her puppy fat — a direct result of her mother's hearty 'meat-and-potatoes' cooking — her appearance and figure improved, melting away the shyness she had lived with all her life. She had dark eyes and jet-black hair and until she started university, wore glasses, but upon arriving she spent her first grant cheque on contact lenses, resulting in a growth in confidence overnight. She was certainly not unattractive and with a pleasant easy-going personality, was popular amongst colleagues and customers.

By the time Jo arrived in Canada, there had been only one boyfriend during her undergraduate days, whom she did not love and in retrospect, questioned whether she even liked. He was also her only sexual encounter; a single occurrence she preferred to forget, but of course could not. Whoever forgets their first? She lost her virginity in a ground-floor bedroom of a student house occupied by five men. The house smelt of damp carpets, body odour and cigarette smoke, as did the sheets of the single bed; sheets she suspected had not been washed for months, if at all. Once it was over, Jo was keen to escape. Walking home with his semen seeping into her underwear, she vowed to end the casual relationship and concentrate on cross-country running; a decision never regretted. The deed was done. She had progressed to 'the other side': she could now move on.

Jo had also never been able to form close bonds with the women she met. When a teenager, she was just part of the crowd, almost an afterthought when it came to parties and social engagements, of which, in her small town, there were few. The girls who did want to be friends she found shallow and petty, frequently opting to avoid them rather than cultivate alliances. During her undergraduate years, she tended to prefer studying or sport to socialising, which was far easier and much less stressful. There had never been a special male, or female friend. Meeting Kate, Andrea and Daphne in Lecture Hall 109 of the Schnolber building and living together was her making. For the first time in her life, she felt valued and supported. It seemed as if they were all on the same page: at long last she had met women she liked and wanted to spend time with. Subsequent accolades in the world of international commerce, and the personal affluence this bought, was not just due to her own hard work and business acumen, but the direct result of the encounter with these three wonderful women, who supported and encouraged her. Her career success was attributable to the relatively new confidence she had with her own being, growing as a direct result of her friendship with Kate, Daphne and Andrea, who became her loudest cheerleaders and greatest advocates, as well as her best friends. One day, she vowed, she would tell them all just what they meant to her if they did not already know.

After completing her master's degree in July 1985, Jo returned to England and started work for Holden Sealants at their North London office. Leaving her friends had not been easy, and during these early days she was lonely, coping with this solitude by throwing herself into work. She had not been at the company long when she met David Morrison, who came to speak to her about the lease of a car. David entered her office, ignored the chair and perched himself on the desk. He was quite good looking, although not particularly tall, and swung his legs revealing pink stripy socks, perfectly matching the colour of his shirt. He confidently announced leasing a car was a big step, not dissimilar to the decision of whether to sleep with a member of the opposite sex. It was important not to make the commitment only to regret it later. Lots of research, David stressed, needed to be undertaken to ensure the model was right, and to establish your body fitted the many features and contours of the machine. This could take a considerable time. David professed he did not want to rush Jo into a decision she would regret. No man had ever paid her such attention.

Before making a commitment to a vehicle, David called to ask her out. Jo was immediately attracted to this flirtatious, confident, funny individual. She accepted the position at Holden Sealants knowing no one. She had no friends other than work colleagues, and a social life limited to visits to the gym, when time permitted, and was therefore keen to generate a social life. Few men had been this attentive, and although his dress sense did seem a little clumsy, his statue slight and his voice loud, she easily forgave these traits. After the first couple of dates, she found herself committed, looking at the telephone, willing it to ring, counting the hours to their next meeting, and spending an inordinate amount of time deciding what to wear; a trait totally out of character. They dated for six months and over the courtship he lavished her with affection. They went on trips to the coast almost every weekend: as soon as one was completed, he was planning the next. He introduced her to his mother but few of his friends, whom, he argued, were too base, only casual acquaintances, stressing that he wanted to keep her to himself. They were married in the spring of 1986 in an intimate ceremony in the small English village where she had been born, attended by Kate, Daphne and Andrea, who made the trans-Atlantic trip specifically for the wedding and were the only female friends of Jo's in attendance.

If asked, Jo would say their marriage, lasting almost twenty-five years, was fine. When pressed by Kate and the others during get-togethers, she reluctantly admitted that David had numerous affairs, describing them as meaningless. These she forgave, believing he did still love her, and deep down she loved him. The acknowledgment of the infidelities occurred in conjunction with a type of acceptance. She understood him best, and after all, he was the only man who had ever told her he loved her or had, indeed, paid her any real attention. And all married men (and many women) have affairs. Was it not something in the male gene which predisposed them to these actions? This interpretation was met with considerable discussion and questioning from her caring cohort, who, in the end, supported Jo and her decision to stay with her husband, even if they did not sanction it. But now things had changed. During the next few days in Las Vegas, Jo would have to reveal what she had discovered.

Last week, while clearing out the spare room in their neat, suburban London home, (financed primarily from her comfortable income), Jo found a dusty box labelled 'Finances 1985'. There, amongst the faded bank statements and yellowing Visa bills, she discovered a receipt from a clinic. It was stapled together with the signed declaration that David was fully aware, in undertaking this procedure, that he was seriously jeopardising his ability to procreate and reversals of the surgery, while possible, were rarely successful. By the time she made this discovery, she was already aware of the affairs. These she tolerated and learned to live with as they never seemed to last long. But this discovery was the ultimate betrayal.

She thought back to the early times in their relationship when they discussed children: all the times, in the initial stages, when they planned together what they would do when she became pregnant, the names they would call the child, how many children they wanted, how they would be schooled, what they would look like. These exciting times eventually gave way to the acknowledgement that conception was not going to be as easy as imagined. There followed numerous stressful visits to doctors and clinics, and countless infertility tests. These examinations were primarily conducted on her body: he was only asked to have his sperm count checked. She remembered the day this was to take place: a cold, wet Saturday in November. That morning, he told her he wanted his best friend, Derek, to accompany him to the clinic for the procedure, not her. At the time she felt hurt, seeing this as odd, but he explained he would be more comfortable attending with a man, when directed to enter the cubical, read the pornographic literature and produce the desired fluid. She acquiesced, accepting his reasoning. Upon reflection, she realised he needed Derek as a stand-in. It was Derek who gave his sperm. Another lie.

Upon accepting she could not easily have children, there followed periods of extreme sadness and many tears. Envious looks at other parents, and the sense that life was unbelievably cruel and unfair. Then followed David's insistence he did not want her, or himself, to go on the emotional rollercoaster of fertility drugs, and medical interventions, followed by his heartfelt convincing and coaxing that they would always love and have each other. She was a successful career woman and would be able to build on this career to make her, and their life, complete. And she totally believed him. He was such a convincing liar, and she so much in love, emotional and gullible. All this time, what she thought was his sensitivity and deep affection towards her was his own totally selfish action. All this time, he knew they could not conceive. The vasectomy had been his insurance that the affairs would not result in a pregnancy. All these years, he had been lying.

For twenty-five years, Jo met her friends who, upon learning of his infidelity, said she should leave him. Their sage advice was non-judgemental. They loved and supported her and were only offering their opinions. She consistently articulated her commitment, reiterating she did still love him, and knew, deep down, that he loved her. A pattern had been formed. This pattern was about to be broken. The forthcoming meeting in Las Vegas would be different. On this occasion, she would tell her girlfriends what she had discovered, and how she now had every intention to not only end her marriage but to curtail all his affairs. At this point in time, she had no idea how this would occur, nor when: she was just adamant she would make it happen and, as always, needed their support.

Kate

The decision of the four to meet in Las Vegas had not been solely influenced by Jo's home-improvement convention. By coincidence, a few days following the hardware show, the American Society of Criminology was holding its annual conference at the Riviera Hotel (a poor cousin to the Hilton, in which Jo was staying) and Kate Thomas had been invited to present a paper, entitled: 'Law Enforcement: Planning for the 2010 Vancouver Winter Olympics — Opportunities and Challenges', a presentation that both excited and scared her. This was the first time, since being promoted to the rank of chief inspector, six months earlier, that she had undertaken anything like this. She had never spoken to an audience of (primarily) academics before. This was out of her comfort zone but provided an exhilarating challenge.

Of the four friends, Kate was undoubtedly the most extrovert, confident, rational and the most secure in herself. The oldest of four daughters, her father was a police officer who had remained in the lower ranks of policing, while her mother was a nurse. Kate grew up on the Canadian Prairies in a small town and finished her degree (History) in the town. She joined the Royal Canadian Mounted Police (RCMP) upon graduation, thereby completing the ambitions her parents had for her. After finishing police training, she was posted to Surrey, the largest municipal RCMP police detachment in Canada, about thirty kilometres south of Vancouver. Aged twenty-one, she therefore moved from rural Canada to a large metropolis and was exposed, for the first time in her life, not only to the concept of a city but to winter temperatures, which were not consistently sub-zero, a relaxed multi-cultural urban environment boasting more than one movie theatre, and an abundance of ethnic cuisines. With a keen ambition and desire to move beyond policing the masses in the rank-and-file role, she quickly sought ways to enhance her career options, so applied and was accepted for the Criminology Master's Degree at UBC. The RCMP encouraged this career-enhancement move, allowing her to attend classes when required. She was also given ten weeks' paid leave, in addition to her standard four weeks holiday, to complete her studies. The Mounties were keen to encourage the pursuit of academic qualifications amongst their members and having a woman wanting to take this option was a bonus. Within the organisation, Kate was already recognised as having potential for management.

Kate had been in Vancouver about eighteen months before commencing her degree, living in a one-bedroom apartment she could ill afford in a trendy area of town. She had recently indulged in the purchase of a yellow VW Beetle car, much to the amusement of her colleagues. This acquisition was made in the full acknowledgment she would become the subject of teasing. Whilst liked and respected amongst her peers, she was also well aware of the dangers of becoming entrenched in the police subculture, and unlike many of her work colleagues, who only socialised with other members of the service professions, Kate was less enamoured with this group and actively sought other social groupings to spend time with. To this extent, she joined numerous book clubs, Pilates classes, cooking courses and regularly attended theatre, although the rigours of shift work and overtime made commitment to these pastimes haphazard, at best. She rarely completed a course, nor formed friendships through these groupings, enjoying them, nonetheless.

As an attractive, confident woman, she both enticed and repelled the opposite sex. Many men found her charisma and confidence unnerving and this, coupled with her five-foot-ten-inch height and chosen career (nice men do not want to date police officers), meant that although there had been a number of boyfriends, quite a few one-night stands and a couple of lovers, none lasted very long. She enjoyed sex and physical contact but had never been in love, and analysed this as her inability to commit. She knew a lot of men, but the majority she saw as shallow and boring; all right for one or two nights, but not long-term. Her best friend, Sarah, whom she had known since kindergarten, and who was still in the house next door to where Kate grew up, saw this interpretation as utterly flawed. In her opinion, men did not commit to Kate because of her overconfidence, and what could be interpreted as dominance and a desire to control. In Sarah's view, all Kate needed to do was let the man have his say, take control and be dominant, then she would find love.

Kate had no problems making friends, albeit on a superficial level, with both sexes: good friends and long-term lovers, however, were a different issue. When asked, Kate never hesitated in saying Sarah was her best friend, but inwardly she knew there was little in common between them now, except the memories of the early days in grade school. The slow, progressive erosion of this relationship started many years ago, probably before high school, when Sarah's ambition was to have a baby and Kate's to become a Mountie. The demise had yet to be acknowledged between the two women. Kate met Jo, Daphne and Andrea at a time when she was searching for contemporaries who were not police officers, and who shared her intellect, interests, beliefs and desire to have fun. Kate did not know it at the time, but Daphne, Jo and Andrea fitted these requirements.

Kate was certainly the most practical of the four women, and on more than one occasion the most abrupt — almost tactless — frequently opening her mouth before thinking who she was about to upset. In her final year at UBC, she had been introduced to Bob de Roche, twelve years her senior and also a Mountie. He was tasked with presenting three lectures on the need for organisational change within the RCMP. These optional lectures were scheduled at nine a.m. Consequently, at the first, Kate found herself one of only four in the seminar. As she explained to Jo, Daphne, and Andrea afterwards, her decision to attend was the best she ever made.

Her attraction to Superintendent De Roche was immediate and intense, unlike anything experienced before. While this forty-year-old man was not physically attractive, his knowledge, charisma and inter-personal skills made reservations about his appearance and age fleeting. Kate fell in love with his nervous laugh, greying hair and six-foot frame, but more importantly, for the first time in her life, she found a man she felt was her intellectual equal and soul mate. A member of the opposite sex who was not afraid to look her in the eye and answer a direct question with a direct answer; a confident man who could admit when he was wrong. She quickly made inquiries and found he was not married. Armed with this knowledge and following a week of intense encouragement from her friends, she resolved, at the end of his second class, to invite him for coffee. Arriving early at the classroom, for the lecture, she discovered she was the only student. It soon became apparent that nine a.m. was too early for her colleagues, who failed to arrive. This fortuitous event meant she had no reason to summon the courage to suggest coffee. He took the initiative, deciding as there was only the two of them, they should relocate to the quiet faculty coffee bar around the corner and conduct an informal lecture from there.

From this date onwards, Kate and Bob were a couple. Jo, Daphne and Andrea took a while to get over the age difference and his somewhat distant, detached manner, but soon came to love and trust him, frequently turning to him for advice and the steady, fatherly hand he offered. For his part, he loved being a part of this female clique. While many men shy away from the feminine gossip their partners engage in, Bob loved being a fly on the wall and relished the opportunity these invites awarded him to learn more about the female being. Andrea referred to him, affectionately, as 'The Fifth Girl'.

Bob and Kate married in 1986, bought a small townhouse in central Vancouver and opted to have dogs, not children. Both were career police officers and remained in the force, gaining promotions and accolades as they grew older. They had a relationship envied and admired. First and foremost, they were best friends, having a deep respect for one another. They shared a passion for the outdoors, especially hiking, cycling, and kayaking, and mutually encouraged each other's ambitions and desires. Theirs was a stable relationship until 2nd May 2009, four days prior to Kate's fiftieth birthday celebration trip to Las Vegas to meet her girlfriends.

Bob had been feeling tired over the course of the previous six months; a physical constraint which seemed to be getting worse. Initially, he attributed this to an increase in workload, as he agreed to take on extra work heading a task force on the recruitment and promotion of ethnic-minority officers within the organisation. Once this was completed, he still felt run-down, finding it increasingly difficult to concentrate, and could not seem to get on top of things, lacking the energy and enthusiasm he always had for his career. Trips to the gym and rides on the bike became out of the question. Kate, of course, noticed this change and spent months gently persuading and finally demanding he see his doctor, which he eventually did, and tests were taken.

On May 2nd, Bob told her, in the calm, collected way so characteristic of him, that he had Lou Gehrig's (motor neurone) disease — or ALS (Amyotrophic Lateral Sclerosis) — and been given between three months and three years to live. His delivery of this news was practical, detached and unemotional, as he had obviously thought it all through before telling her, being more concerned over Kate's wellbeing than his own demise. He explained to her the advantages the terminally ill have: the death can be planned and the family and loved ones are spared the sudden shock, and all can gradually become accustomed to the consequences. Bob quietly outlined that, over the course of the next few months, he would lose the ability to use his limbs, but his mind would not be affected. He would remain at home for as long as he could, not wanting to move to a hospice to die.

Kate sat and listened in total disbelief over what she was hearing, holding his hand as tears silently streamed down her face. This was not supposed to happen. Bob continued, obviously having thought about the forthcoming sequence of events. He was fully aware she had recently been promoted and, in her new role as chief inspector, and involvement with the forthcoming Vancouver Olympics, needed to be free from this emotional rollercoaster and from him. He was going to die — it may as well be sooner than later — and therefore he wanted Kate to aid his suicide. It was only at this point, as the words slowly left his lips, that she recognised how scared he was. Kate immediately protested. She was a police officer; he was a police officer. Not only was this act illegal, she could not do it. They should not do it. Bob calmly said he did not expect her to do it by herself, but thought with help, and the support of her girlfriends, she would be able to.

She knelt by him, holding his hand to her lips while he leant into her hair and started to sob. She had never seen him cry before and through the sobs, he pleaded with her not to let him die in pain. How could she not agree to this? She vowed she would help with his suicide, allowing him to die with dignity, under his terms, considerate of his wishes, before the pain became extreme.

Six days later, Kate kissed Bob goodbye after he drove her to Vancouver Airport for her flight to Las Vegas, leaving her to consider whether she was going to ask her friends to assist her with the suicide of her husband, or whether she would do it by herself. One thing was for sure: she would carry out the wishes of the only man she had ever loved and now, more than ever before, she desperately needed the counsel and support of her friends to do this.

Daphne

Daphne Faith never had a problem with men committing, or even overcommitting. Her first marriage proposal came two weeks after dating her first boyfriend, when she was sixteen (unless, of course, you count the one from her father's alcoholic best friend when she was fourteen), and since that time there had been others. Men fell in love with Daphne with amazing regularity. After one date, frequently arranged by her older sister, they were hooked, even if she was not. With her exceptional good looks — which included long, natural blonde hair, blue eyes and an hourglass figure — she was often mistaken as the clichéd dizzy blonde, having the insight to play on this interpretation when it suited, using it to her advantage. There was another side however: she was serious, studied life and analysed events to the extent that, more than once, she had been described as 'wise beyond her years'. She was also very shy — a trait which existed well into her twenties — liked reading poetry and spent considerable periods of time in her own company. Consequently, she found making friends difficult. For Daphne, solitude was a normal situation, but this was an involuntary solitude, not a chosen one; an isolation which frequently led to loneliness.

Daphne was incredibly smart and found gaining a place at Law School far easier than she had been led to believe it would be. If honest, she did not really know if she wanted to be a lawyer, but could not think of an alternative, so opted for UBC. The daughter of affluent parents, who separated when she was twelve years old, she had grown up in Vancouver, negotiating time between two homes, and the tense relationships which coexisted between them; a circumstance adding to her maturity. Dividing time between two households and acting as a buffer between warring parents meant growing up quickly. During the week, she attended a girl's boarding school, which she disliked, but tolerated without too many questions or adolescent outbursts. She had taken her first degree in Vancouver in English Literature, and despite having travelled extensively in Europe and Asia with her mother and sister, and having the income to study wherever she wanted, she had no desire to live or pursue an advanced degree abroad.

In 1983, at the age of twenty-one, she found forging relationships difficult, especially those with women, and hated thinking she did not have a 'best friend', as all other women seemed to, feeling like she had failed in some crucial task, that everyone else, by her age, had succeeded in. On numerous occasions she found herself sitting alone in coffee bars, covertly watching women gossip and giggle together, feeling pangs of immense jealousy, knowing she had never felt this bond, being at a loss to comprehend it. Although close to her older sister, she wondered if this was only because there existed no other women whom she could fully understand and tolerate. She envied the gossip other women thrived upon, but also often found it to be trivial and uninteresting. Consequently, Daphne had difficulty embracing women of her age who seemed to be immature, mirroring the men who found her attractive, preferring to retreat into her own company.

Always a deep thinker, prior to meeting Kate, Jo and Andrea, Daphne was so concerned over her inability to make friends that she spent a week in the public library, researching the subject of friendships in academic, psychological journals where the issue was empirically investigated by noted professionals. There, she found a study showing that, on average, human beings have three categories of friends. The first is limited to five 'intimate relationships' — contacts who would be called on in the time of crisis; the second, a group consisting of approximately fifteen close friends and family, who are seen regularly; and the final group consisted of good friends who would be invited to a party and may be as great as fifty in number. At that time, Daphne felt she had only one individual as an intimate friend — her older sister. The other women she knew were little more than acquaintances. She questioned if they could even be included in the third group. This situation changed upon meeting Kate, Jo and Andrea.

Daphne remained at UBC two years longer than the others in the completion of her law degree and in those final years, she missed the company and support the other three offered. True, Andrea and Kate were in Vancouver and she saw them regularly, but it was not the same. In the summer of 1988, Daphne left UBC and started to article with a large corporate law firm in Vancouver, a position she found no difficulty acquiring. Quickly, her social life developed into a series of after-work drinking sessions — some just lasting a brief hour; others stretching into the early hours of the following day. While somewhat on the periphery, it was during one of these work-initiated gatherings that she was introduced to Kevin, a lawyer from another office who, at first, seemed quite reserved, but who dressed well, spoke quietly, and was courteous and polite when he talked with her. He had very blond hair — nearly white — and a serious expression, almost sullen and aloof. He tended to hang back on the edges of a group but was regularly the last to leave. Like her, he seemed to have few people to talk to.

In contrast to the other men Daphne had met, Kevin did not shower her with attention but cultivated a cool, distant persona. Daphne learned he had been married and divorced twice, even though he was only a few years older than her. One colleague explained he was not good with relationships but when pressed did not expand, suggesting Daphne should not find out. Daphne did not like being told what to do, and for the first time in her life found it necessary to be proactive in the pursuit of a man. Aged twenty-nine, she was also keen to lose her virginity, which hung like a noose around her neck. Kevin, she believed, would be an ideal candidate to address this task.

For the following four years, Daphne had an on-again/off-again relationship with Kevin, which came as little surprise to her colleagues. The fantastic 'on-again' periods were the times he was not drinking, involving intimate dinners, walks on the beach, weekends away and a lot of physical sex. The 'off-again' times were when the drinking binges took over; the slamming of doors, the loud, circular arguments and the hurtful words resulting in vows to end the relationship and never see him again; vows easily broken, similar to episodes she remembered from her own parents' marriage.

In 1991, when Daphne turned thirty-two, her father died leaving her with a considerable sum of money and letting her question the fragile nature of the relationships everyone has with those they love or profess to love. At this juncture, Daphne realised she had been in a four-year relationship that needed either to be ended or confirmed by marriage. By this time a successful lawyer, she remained unsure and apprehensive about her relationships with men. At thirty-two, she concluded if Kevin did not want to marry her, perhaps no one else would, and consequently she would not have the children she craved, nor take on the role of wife. This thought scared her, especially as Jo, Andrea and Kate were already married, making her the odd one out. Although none of them commented on this, she found she became preoccupied with her single state. Just as in the past she watched women in coffee bars bond with other women, and wondered at this relationship, now she found herself looking for wedding rings and questioning why others were married and she was not. While acknowledging many marriages were not good, the bond and public statement personified by the ring stated to the world that you belonged. Someone loved you enough to want to always be with you. Irrationally, she explained away Kevin's bouts of alcoholism as inconvenient but surmountable. After all, many of his friends did not know he had a problem with drink, and only a couple of years ago he was promoted to senior partner at his firm, tripling his salary, so surely it could not be that bad. People changed with marriage and when they became parents, she reasoned, and he did profess to want children. Kevin had not proposed or even suggested they live together, although at least four nights a week they were in each other's apartments, and the status of established couple was accepted, if not fully understood, by all who knew them. His former relationships were acknowledged, but never discussed in detail, and Daphne did not want to go there: what he had done when younger was of no consequence now.

Daphne broached the subject of marriage one Sunday morning after a particularly playful early-morning sex session. She had not planned the conversation and when she asked him to marry her, it surprised her just as much as it did him. He accepted without discussion and then held her very tightly for a long time, not saying a word. When recalling this event to her friends, the emotion which stayed in her memory was her overwhelming desire to escape the embrace and pee.

They were married in 1994 and ten months later had the first of three children, who, in Daphne's fiftieth year, were fourteen, thirteen and eleven. Daphne never returned to work, instead throwing herself into the role of mother. She totally adored her children. Unlike many women who give up careers to nurture offspring and secretly regret it, Daphne loved her children and enjoyed every stage of their developing lives. She was on every school parent committee, spent her life chauffeuring them to sports events, swimming lessons, games, theatre activities, concerts, music lessons and play dates. As Kevin's drinking became more frequent — justified, he stated, because of the pressures of work — Daphne dedicated considerable periods of time ensuring her children did not spend long with their father. She watched herself making a string of excuses for him; excuses which her offspring, as they grew older, increasingly started to question. And Kevin showed little interest in the lives of his children as they aged. For the last six years, all attended boarding school on Vancouver Island, a three-hour journey from their home, in an attempt by Daphne to keep the truth from them about their father, his addiction, and subsequent violent behaviour. This separation hurt her, but she knew it was for their own good, remembering how she hated being exposed to her parents' seemingly endless, alcohol-induced arguments when a child.

A few days prior to Daphne's planned departure for Las Vegas, Kevin arrived home, drunk, in the early hours of the morning. At two a.m., he entered their bedroom and threw his now huge, middle-aged frame on top of her. It had been three weeks since he last physically assaulted her and the bruises had only just gone. Following that attack, Daphne stayed home for five days, waiting for them to fade sufficiently to be disguised by make-up. She could not let the same events take place again. She quickly rolled out from under him and ran to the bathroom, locking the door, spending the next six hours on the cold, tiled bathroom floor.

She spent the night in the confined space, sobbing, running over the options for her and the children, vividly remembering how she grew up between two divorced parents. The idea of joint custody would mean he would have more access than he currently did. For them to develop into normal human beings, they did not need divorced parents, especially when one was an abusive alcoholic. To her knowledge, Kevin had never laid a hand on the children, but Daphne could not be sure this would not happen, especially as they reached the rebellious teenage years. But she could not stay. There was only one option, her exhausted consciousness told her: he would have to go. She would have to think of a way of killing him. At first, the thought repelled her but during the night on the bathroom floor, she rationalised it to be the only way out. An accident needed to happen, resulting in his death. She finally slept a little and upon hearing his car pull out of the driveway, unlocked the bathroom door, her body aching from the cold floor she had endured. Entering the kitchen to make coffee, Daphne reflected on the night, starting to giggle while recalling her extreme, emotional, night-time intentions. Thank goodness she would soon have the counsel of Kate, Jo and Andrea to add some rationality to what were obviously the tired, alcohol-induced, perimenopausal thoughts of a deranged fifty-year-old woman. Killing abusive partners was the subject of television murder mysteries, not those of an intelligent, rational, middle-class mother.

A few days later, she scribbled a note to Kevin, telling him she was going away, and taped it to the fridge, then took a taxi to Vancouver Airport. After checking in, she went to sit in Starbucks in the prearranged rendezvous location where she had agreed to meet Andrea. She had purposely dressed casually for the trip, knowing that Andrea, unlike the rest of the group, looked every one of her fifty years, and did not have the same amount of money as the others to spend in attempting to slow the aging process. She ordered her non-fat latte and headed towards the bar stools, unfolded her magazine, and sat down. Daphne looked up when she heard footsteps approaching fast. It was her friend, who seemed agitated: she was crying yet laughing at the same time.

'I'm in love again,' Andrea announced, bouncing into the stool adjacent to Daphne's, then put her head in her hands and started to sob. Daphne rested her hands on her friend's shoulder.

'It's going to be one of those weeks,' she thought. 'But how I love the emotions of these women.'

Andrea

Andrea Sealy was not very tall, and a little top-heavy. She constantly fought to keep her weight below 150lbs, rarely managing to succeed. Her grandparents, on her mother's side, immigrated to Canada from Japan in the 1930s, and as a genetic result she had straight black hair and very dark eyes; almost an exotic look. During her childhood she had a fiery temper but in growing older, this softened considerably: consequently, with age, she became more popular amongst her peers. A caring, light-hearted girl, not deep or moody but contemplative; a girl who, from an early age, knew what she wanted and had her life planned out. Having a good sense of humour, she was seen to be a fun person to have around, and caring, sensitive and thoughtful. She had grown up in a small rural community seven hundred kilometres away from Vancouver, where her parents both worked for the City Council in administrative jobs. She had two siblings, twelve and fourteen years older than she was. Both left home before she reached the age of ten, and although living in the same town, she saw little of them. As a family, they were not close. They did not tend to talk about anything deep or address any subjects which could cause embarrassment or be upsetting; a trait not questioned while growing up.

Andrea completed her education and subsequent nursing qualifications in the town where she was born. Many of her teachers suggested she pursue a more academic path, as she was certainly able to, but Andrea saw no benefit in this. She wanted to work in a caring profession, and stay in the familiar environment with the people she knew and liked, and who understood her. No one in her social circle moved away and her parents did little to encourage it. There was no role model suggesting life elsewhere was better. Ambition beyond the confines of the town was an alien concept. Her town was the kind of place where everyone knew everyone else, which Andrea only saw to be a positive thing, seeing no reason not to do like many others had done here: grow up, get married, settle down, have children and age amongst friends in the familiar, safe surroundings she saw as home. She liked the routine and the security this offered. She did not seek, nor want change or excitement.

Ever since she could remember, Andrea had known Brad Pointer. They attended the same school, although he was a couple of grades higher. His parents ran the local hardware store, and as Andrea's father was perpetually trying to fix things, and escape from the house — more specifically from his wife and her Catholic teachings — Andrea and her father knew the shop intimately. Some of Andrea's earliest memories were visits to the store with her dad. Here, she could perch on a stool at the corner of the shop, out of sight of most people, and eat popcorn — which Brad's father supplied to his customers at no charge — while her father spent eternities searching for the correct screw, nail or bolt he needed for the specific job in hand, chatting to the endless stream of men who entered the store and who, like him, saw no urgency to leave this warm, welcoming man-cave.

Growing older, it was not the popcorn that was the main draw, but Brad, who helped his father on weekends. Over the course of time, the two young people started to exchange nervous grins, growing to limited conversations, and subsequently, gentle teasing. By the time she started high school, they were an established couple amongst their peers. Both were seen as 'nice kids', volunteering at local community events, regularly attending church, working hard at school, being polite to the people they met, and not getting into any trouble. They did everything together. Andrea not only saw him as her boyfriend, but as her best friend, providing the support her parents were unwilling to give.

As the town in which they lived was small, Andrea and Brad existed in a cohort of teenage friends, sharing many social events within this tight-knit group. But Andrea was aware she did not share much with her own sex. She could talk to Brad about everything, so she confided in him: he was the one who really understood her. He was special. While she was popular, having several female friends, it was Brad who understood her best; not these chattering gossiping females whom, if pressed, she admitted she tolerated, but often found tedious and immature.

As an only child, Brad was being groomed to work at the store, so upon leaving school he simply rolled his weekend job into a full-time one. He was a sociable young man with many friends, but little ambition outside regular ice hockey games in the winter, and baseball matches in the summer. Like Andrea, he was happy within the confines of the town. Andrea also recognised that her life with Brad would be centred within this community and was totally content with this, until an event took place changing this view, and her destiny.

Andrea had taken her nurse training at the local hospital and additional classes in the nearby community college. As part of her final year of training, she was required to spend three months at another hospital, so briefly moved to Vancouver, and spent her secondment at BC Women's Hospital. This necessitated living away from home for the first time in her life. Although returning home on a couple of weekends, this period was her first taste of real independence. Andrea was well liked by her colleagues and superiors during the secondment, and despite being asked to stay and build a career in Vancouver, was impatient to get back to her familiar life, which she missed, to qualify and take up a promised position at the local hospital, where she knew everyone and had undertaken most of her training. This was the well-thought-out plan ever since she could remember. Brad barely touched on the subject of marriage, but she, and many others in town, as well as their Catholic families, presumed that within a couple of years they would be wed and settle down in the only community they knew, ready to mirror the lives of both sets of parents.

She qualified and had been at her new job at the local hospital only six weeks when Brad told her he intended to end the relationship and was going to marry Kathy Johnson, whom he had a somewhat brief, yet physical affair with while Andrea was in Vancouver, and who was now pregnant. Andrea was devastated. This was not just another girl: this girl was supposed to be one of her closest friends. She was one of their 'group', whom Andrea had known since kindergarten. She suspected nothing and neither Brad nor Kathy implied, in any of their past actions, that there was anything between them. All Andrea's dreams were in ruins. To make matters worse, a large, elaborate Catholic marriage ceremony was being planned and would take place in town. She would be expected to encounter Brad and Kathy on numerous occasions for the rest of her life. Within two days of receiving the news, she secured a transfer to BC Women's Hospital in Vancouver, which provided accommodation and enabled her to start work the following month. She then said an unemotional goodbye to her parents, and boarded the Greyhound bus with one suitcase.

Many in her small town, including her parents, thought she would be back, but this hurt and the betrayal — not only of her one and only boyfriend but also of a close friend and, by implication, other friends — made her adamant her future was to be elsewhere.

Not long after arriving in Vancouver and meeting Kate, Jo, and Daphne, Andrea met Peter, a physiotherapist, also working at BC Women's Hospital. Peter was a quiet, sensitive man with a genuine caring nature and, like Andrea, Catholic. Not much taller than Andrea, slightly younger and a little rotund, his main passion was field hockey, which he played three nights a week after work, and making models with Lego. Andrea thought the sport fun, but presumed boys grew out of Lego when they were about twelve. Obviously, this was not the case. Peter introduced her to a small circle of adult enthusiasts, mostly men, whom she enjoyed and found entertaining. She quickly came to appreciate his passion, although not fully understand it. Peter had been bought up in the Catholic faith, so they had religion in common, although they shared the same questionable level of commitment. He believed in contraception, but was passionately opposed to divorce; an opinion conveyed to Andrea in no uncertain terms by his mother and sisters, whom he was close to.

Peter was totally different to Brad. He was not 'one of the boys'; completely impractical when it came to fixing anything, but could cook exceptionally well and was an avid reader, often arriving late for a date with the excuse being he had become engrossed in the latest science-fiction book or fantasy novel. He did not have a wide circle of friends but was always pleasant and sociable when out. He was a very safe person. On their second date, he admitted Andrea was his first girlfriend, and on their fifth date, two weeks after they first set eyes on each other, and with their physical contact being confined to a few clumsy kisses, he suggested — in a somewhat off-hand, practical way — they should consider marriage.

Reflecting on this rapid course of events, twenty-five years later, Andrea readily acknowledged she was on the rebound, and desperately wanted to let Brad and Kathy and everyone in her home town know she had moved on, and was not upset over the turn of events. Establishing a friendship group with Kate, Jo and Daphne — all women who seemed so much more confident and attractive — also led to pressure, never stated, that it would be Andrea, who would be the one men were not attracted to. She thought of herself as the clichéd ugly duckling of the group, and although no one would articulate it, she did not have the physical appearance or defining attributes of the others. Daphne was the true beauty; Jo, although not a model, was not over-weight, nor was she small or shy; and Kate was so tall and confident, she turned heads just because of it. In her hometown, being small and carrying a few extra pounds did not seem to matter as much as it did in the big city. Peter's kind nature and attentiveness served to negate, if not completely banish, doubts she had about her physical appearance and confidence, and helped her to forget the first love of her life. Peter saw her as a person and was not concerned over what she looked like, or what she wore, or her personal style. He appreciated her for herself. And she was attracted to him: he was a great listener, interesting, and fun to be with. He also provided the structure she craved.

Andrea nervously introduced her girlfriends to her new boyfriend in a small vegetarian restaurant. They crammed around the table clearly designed for four and Peter answered all questions, laughed at jokes, subtly teased each one of them in succession, fitting in perfectly. Afterwards, the women enthused over this new-found love. They, of course, had been told about Brad, and actively encouraged Andrea's new relationship in a supportive way, as true friends do. Just before Jo returned to England, Peter and Andrea were married in Vancouver, in a small Catholic church. Her parents attended but were the only ones invited from her hometown.

Peter had been completely honest with Andrea, telling her from the outset that he did not want to have children; a sentiment she genuinely believed would change as he grew older, with pressure from his mother and because of his faith. But he had a stubborn streak: his view did not alter and like so many issues in their relationship, she was reluctant to venture into this explosive area. They were not particularly physical, and if honest, she would say she thought he did not actually enjoy sex, or even touching her. He would never initiate any physical contact and in the early days, when she suggested it, there was often an excuse — he was too tired, needed a shower, had something more pressing to do — so after a while, she stopped asking. After five years of marriage, sex was an exceedingly rare occurrence. At first this bothered her, but as the years passed, she accepted it. They had a good relationship as friends, he was kind to her and interesting and they got on well, enjoying each other's company. She liked living with him and sharing a life with him. It would have been nice to have some form of intimacy, but this was not a deal breaker.

It was while on a holiday in Cuba, following an evening of mojito cocktails in a romantic environment, when he was unable to find an excuse, that they had rapid, drunken sex. Andrea found an old condom in her toiletries bag, and they used it, but immediately afterwards discovered it had split. Any thoughts Andrea had of post-orgasmic affection were shattered as Peter quickly left the bedroom, cursing, confirming to Andrea he was still adamant he did not want to parent a child. Andrea, however, was excited and tilted her pelvis, holding the position for the next forty-five minutes until she needed to use the washroom, attempting to ensure his semen reached the destination it was intended for. It did. She successfully conceived but did not tell him until she was over four-months pregnant, ensuring she could have the child she craved. Their daughter, Amy, was born in 2000, when Andrea was forty-one.

All the way through their marriage, Andrea maintained Peter was a good husband and despite claiming not to want children, an excellent father. As the years progressed, however, she found she had less and less in common with him. Since Amy was born, they had not had sex and barely any physical contact. They lived together civilly, never discussing this situation. To an increasing extent, their social life and interests did not involve each other, but this was of no consequence. If Andrea had any doubts about her marriage, these were suppressed, and she received comfort thinking of her colleagues, many of whom also seemed to be in the same sort of sexless relationship. She adored Amy and the close bond they had developed. Questions she had about Peter were negated by her adoration for her child. This bond was unshakeable — there was nothing she would not do for Amy — but as the time passed, she knew this closeness would wain, as Amy would want to build on her own life; a life which would not include a leading role for her mother.

It was New Year's Eve in 2008, just before the night's celebrations, when Andrea entered the small box room regarded as Peter's domain. Most men have sheds or garages to keep their 'boy toys' or hobbies: for Peter, it was a small room where he stored neatly catalogued boxes of Lego and hockey equipment, and where bookshelves covered the walls, housing his favourite novels. Andrea rarely went into this space, but upon opening the door, that day, she found him sobbing in the chair.

'What on earth is wrong?' she exclaimed, taking his hands, and kneeling at his side. This was so out of character. He swallowed hard and told her, without any hesitation, that he was gay, had always been gay, and could no longer go on living a lie. He broke down, apologising over and over again, until she said it did not matter and left the room to find a quiet room in which to digest the news and decide what, if anything, she needed to do.

The following months were exceedingly difficult, as neither broached the subject. At times, it seemed as if that fateful day had not occurred, that it had been a weird fantasy she dreamed up and that the confession did not take place. During this time, she grew to accept Peter's homosexuality, something maybe always suspected, but denied to herself and others. She would never be able to tell Amy, knowing he would not want her to. When Amy left home, Andrea told herself, would be the correct time for her to change her life and leave Peter. She still loved him in her own way, but maybe in her later years would need a partner who would love her physically. Despite everything, she cared deeply for Peter: they had shared a lot, and after Jo, Kate and Daphne, he was her best friend and that would never change.

In May 2009, Andrea arrived early at Vancouver Airport. She did not much care for flying but was looking forward to the three hours she would have with Daphne and the gossip during the flight to Las Vegas. She admired and adored this woman, who was always full of surprises, sensitive, humorous and entertaining. Andrea had spent the previous six months saving hard for the trip and was nervous and excited. She would have loved to have taken Amy, and half-promised she would do, to celebrate her eighteenth birthday, but that was far in the future. Now was the time for herself and her friends.

Andrea, Kate and Daphne all lived in Vancouver but work, families and domestic commitments meant the three of them met up only about three times a year, usually for lunch, and it always seemed a little odd to do it with three and not four. It was Jo's home-improvement show gatherings which took place over days and nights, when the bonding and reaffirmation of their love for one another took place.

The taxi dropped Andrea at the domestic departure gates, not the USA departures, requiring her to walk the length of the terminal to find Alaska Airways. The airport was busy with people searching for fast-food outlets, departure gates and baggage drops, paying little attention to the sea of other passengers. Andrea blended into the crowd, and as she did, thought she recognised the man walking towards her. She stopped, staring at him. He looked sad, tired and was about to walk straight past her when she spoke his name, almost under her breath. Brad. His eyes flickered towards her and then his expression immediately changed, speaking her name slowly, but with the same affection as when he last pronounced it, almost twenty years ago. Then he took hold of both her hands in his and lifted each one in turn to his lips. There was no shyness or reservation, and she did not resist. He then flung his arms around her, held her very tightly and repeated over again, 'I was so wrong. So, so wrong. Please forgive me.' Taking her hand, they clumsily navigated other passengers, and their luggage, as he led her to a galley of wooden steps acting as resting places, covered with seated travellers looking at the huge, green, jade Bill Reid sculpture. Sitting her down amongst the throng, he quickly explained how his marriage ended ten years ago, and Kathy had moved away; his parents (like hers) were dead, but he remained in the same place, at the hardware store. With emotion in his voice, he said there was not a day that went by when he did not think of her and the huge mistake he made.

Still holding his hand and also fighting back tears, Andrea quickly conveyed the significant events in her life, including the fact that she was married and about to catch a plane for Vegas to celebrate her fiftieth birthday with her three closest friends, none, of course, whom he knew. He asked for her phone number, but she refused to give it to him, nor her married name, but did agree to take his, and promised at some point in the next ten years she would call, already calculating it could take that time to terminate her marriage, see her daughter grow to adulthood, and radically change her life to include him.

Las Vegas

Jo had booked a table at a busy restaurant on the Las Vegas Strip, the day the trade show finished. It was agreed they would all meet there at seven p.m. Kate's conference was at the Riviera, which was an older hotel on the Strip. She had a room at this hotel for herself and Andrea. Daphne, for whom money was not an issue, was staying in her own room at the Hilton. Although the ground floor of the restaurant was noisy, Jo knew the upstairs balcony overlooking the Strip was quieter, cooler and an ideal location for girl bonding.

The National Hardware Show finished at three p.m. but, as was always the case with three-day shows, nothing happened in the final few hours, so it was possible to start slowly dismantling the exhibition booth. An edifice that had taken the best part of two days to assemble was reduced to bare bones within a couple of hours. The shipping agents tasked with removing all the boxes of displays had not arrived by five thirty p.m., so Jo assigned a junior colleague to wait, and returned to the adjacent Hilton for a quick shower and to change from her power suit to a more comfortable cocktail dress. Having been busy thinking of existing clients, new sales leads, and promoting products for the expanding South America markets, Jo had spent little time anticipating the forthcoming three nights and four days with her friends.

Stepping out of the shower, Jo heard a knock on the door. Draping a towel around her body and removing the plastic shower cap, she ran to open it, knowing it would be Daphne. Her friend stood there, looking like a Gucci advertisement. With her children at boarding school, a comfortable inheritance and a husband employed as a senior partner in a prestigious law firm, Daphne spent her days at the gym and shopping, in addition to a few volunteer hours working at the hospice store. Money was not an issue. Jo flung her arms around Daphne and her towel dislodged.

'It's been so long,' she gasped.

'I know,' said Daphne, looking down at the damp mark on her silk blouse, a little uncomfortable over the display of wet affection. Quickly moving into the large suite, she kicked off her pink stilettoes and threw her purse on the bed. 'Good show?' she asked.

'Think so,' said Jo. 'I have hundreds of business cards and with the economy turning, it certainly seems we are on for another bumper year.' Jo re-entered the bathroom and started to brush her hair while Daphne moved to the wardrobe, to critically explore the contents.

'You should wear this,' she ordered, taking a green sleeveless dress from its hanger, holding it against herself. Jo wrinkled her nose.

'Whatever I wear, I will not be able to compete with your attire! My God, how I wish you would get that flabby menopausal body the rest of us have developed.'

'You do not have a menopausal body, do you?' responded Daphne, playfully tugging at Jo's towel.

The banter continued as Jo quickly finished applying make-up, exiting the bathroom to discreetly find underwear, while Daphne was exploring the mini fridge, and then stepped into the green dress to complete the preparations.

'You cannot have a drink! We need to make tracks. I was going to suggest walking until I saw your heels,' Jo exclaimed.

'No way! It's a cab or nothing. These puppies are just for show, not function,' Daphne replied, putting on the shoes.

The taxi dropped them off a little before seven p.m., and they walked into the bar just as a semi-naked woman slid down inside a large glass slide, from the floor above, to the bar. They took the stairs to the third floor, where Andrea and Kate were already waiting. There followed five minutes of four women talking at once. Kisses, hugs, comments over new haircuts and new hair colours, weight loss (but not gains) and clothes, culminating in the conclusion that really no one looked any older than the previous year. A skinny, thirteen-year-old waitress observed these activities with the 'whatever' bubble hanging over her head. She tried to identify a gap in the conversation to suggest drinks and present menus, but after a couple of attempts she decided to leave this group, who, she thought, really were too old to be here, and reappear after she had given her attention to the six young men at the corner table, who undoubtedly would be better tippers and were far better eye candy.

There was, of course, no formality or nervousness as all enthused over being in Las Vegas and congratulated Jo on finding another fantastic location for their bonding session. Daphne got up, found the thirteen-year-old employee, and discretely ordered champagne while the others chattered. When it arrived, she flippantly stated it was her treat and there was to be no arguing. Enjoying the wine as they shared a plate of nachos, each woman basked in the experience of being with old friends they loved, who loved them back, and knew so well.

As the evening unfolded, Jo told them of the trade show and her career successes, Daphne described the plight of bringing up three teenagers and Andrea entertained, as she always did, with tales of life in a hospital and stories of leaving old ladies, already with wizened skin, in the bath too long so they come out with even more wrinkles; finding two male doctors in the laundry room together; and the orderly's first day, when he was dispatched with an amputated leg only to put it down the laundry shoot, not the body parts shoot, causing a two-thousand-dollar 'mistake'. No one chose to discuss husbands. This was the pattern of these regular meetings: no one explicitly stated the subject was taboo, but there was a tacit understanding that too many emotions could be unleashed if this topic was raised prematurely. The women needed time to build up and reaffirm the bond before difficult subjects were introduced.

As time wore on, an additional three bottles of wine, as well as the champagne, were consumed. At midnight, Jo suggested they should go. Ignored by Daphne and Andrea, who were deep in a drunken, animated conversation over the unfathomable dress sense of teenage girls, she turned to Kate, realising she had been uncharacteristically quiet during the evening.

'Everything good?' she said, in an off-hand way.

Kate stared back, saying, 'He's going to die,' as her eyes filled with tears. Daphne and Andrea stopped their dialogue with an almost sixth sense, turning their attention to Kate. Kate swallowed and held Jo's gaze.

'He has Lou Gherig's disease and been given a maximum of three years, and he doesn't want to suffer so he wants me to help him to die. He wants me to kill him and I can't do it by myself. Can you help me?'

Daphne, Jo and Andrea glanced nervously at each other for a second, then Andrea got up and moved around the table, tears already falling from her cheeks, put her arms around Kate's neck and whispered, 'Of course we will. Bob is the fifth girl and if it's what he and what you want, we will be there.'

At this point Kate started to sob and, not for the first time, the waitress decided to leave the table of women alone, thinking of the town's motto: 'What happens in Vegas, stays in Vegas.'

Chapter 2
With Glowing Hearts
Vancouver, Winter Olympics 2010

Since returning to England from her academic studies in Vancouver in 1985, Jo had visited this beautiful West Coast city on seven separate occasions, primarily to see her girlfriends. Unfortunately, the core of the Canadian home-improvement industry was in the cities of Toronto and Montreal in Eastern Canada so, to date, there had been little business reason for her to stay in the west. Jo loved Vancouver, not only because of these girlfriends, who were perpetually telling her to relocate here, but because it was the place that taught her to grow. In Vancouver she transformed into a confident capable woman, shedding her insecurities. Vancouver was the catalyst to her change, to her growing up, to becoming the person she was, and to forming the strong friendship ties relied upon today.

In 2003, Vancouver was awarded the 2010 Winter Olympics, beating Pyeongchang, South Korea and Salzburg, Austria. The city of Berne in Germany was also in contention, but a referendum in September 2002 found the citizens of that city unsupportive of the bid. Prior to throwing its hat into the ring, many in

Vancouver felt the city could ill afford the expense and should be addressing more pressing social issues, such as poverty and the lack of affordable housing. Vancouver held a referendum in February 2003, achieving 64% support.

Almost immediately after winning the Olympic bid, numerous businesses were actively engaged in securing the lucrative sponsorship rights. As one of the largest home improvement retail stores in Canada, The Building Box, a large building-supply store, was quick to secure one of these. With significant sales, this Montreal-based retailer, boasting over one hundred stores across the country, was one of her company's key accounts. Jo knew the advertising and exposure during the Vancouver Olympics would help considerably in the promotion of the Holden Sealant's name and brand, especially to the burgeoning Latin America market, and of course would not hinder growth in existing markets. Jo, therefore, had no hesitation arguing to her CEO, Bernard Trim, and the financial department, that Holden Sealants be involved in as many ways as possible in supporting The Building Box's sponsorship of the Vancouver Olympic Games. Jo was planning to spend the first few weeks of February 2010 in Vancouver with two divergent objectives: to plan Holden Sealants' sales activities prior to and during the Games, and to help a man to die.

Although diagnosed with ALS in 2009, with the possibility of three years to live, Kate's husband, Bob, was becoming progressively weaker. He could no longer climb, unassisted, down the stairs of the townhouse he shared with Kate, so the bedroom had been relocated downstairs in what was their spacious study. This was a bright room with patio doors overlooking the waters of the Burrard Inlet, awarding a relaxing, therapeutic view. Despite Bob's illness, Kate continued to work, being actively involved with the security and planning for the forthcoming Olympics. She soon discovered this demanded little policing expertise, but did require significant managerial and organisational skills, together with an ability to walk a political tightrope. Diplomacy was needed, in great amounts, to deal with the supportive interest groups who were watering their egos at the Olympic trough, as well as those who were ardently against it; particularly the anti-poverty and First Nations activists who believed the significant Olympic budget should be spent on more pressing local social issues, such as affordable housing.

Over one thousand additional police officers were being drafted into Vancouver for the Games, with all Vancouver police officers denied overtime and holidays throughout the event. The local media announced that three cruise ships were to be positioned in the harbour to accommodate the additional security staff. Consequently, Kate found herself responding to controversial publicity telling of police officers being housed on luxury cruise ships at the expense of the

Canadian taxpayer. Security was a highly contentious issue: originally budgeted at one million Canadian dollars, it grew to eventually reach five million Canadian dollars (approximately four million United States dollars).

Kate's time also involved regular press briefings to extinguish the unanticipated fires that flared up daily. Every morning, leaving Bob became harder. He did have friends who wanted to see him. The Royal Canadian Mounted Police, like police agencies across the globe, have a strong supportive subculture, and Bob was well-liked and respected, but every visit he found more tiring. Nurses, doctors, social workers, and various health professionals also called throughout the day to monitor his decline. Kate knew this dignified man was just marking time: his fate had been decided and his rational mind knew this.

She quickly learned that ALS was an exceptionally cruel disease, eroding the body and its abilities, but preserving the brain and all cognitive functions. The victim comprehends exactly what is happening, while observing their body's slow decay. Kate recognised Bob was rapidly approaching the time he wanted to end his life. The pain was increasing. She knew this six-foot man, whom she adored, hated asking for her assistance to be helped to the washroom, loathed being spoon-fed, and found his dependence on her to be shaved, washed and moved to a wheelchair degrading. Being so dependent on others, the contrast between his current existence and his former independent life could not have been more extreme. Terminal illnesses, such as cancer or ALS, were never on Bob's, nor Kate's, agenda. These illnesses happened to others, occurred to characters in films or books or newspapers: known of but awarded little thought. But now everything had changed. The new normal had to be accepted, and with this there was the knowledge that the state was only going to get worse, as was the pain.

Each of the weekly appointments with the specialist at the hospital took longer to navigate and after every visit, Bob was quieter and more reflective. He hated the well-meaning, sympathetic looks from able-bodied strangers when exposed to the outside world; a world now seen only from the seated position of a wheelchair. Kate saw the pain on his face as he sought out the easily accessible washrooms, navigated tight corners and steered towards smooth pavements. There was never good news. How can you give good news to someone terminally ill?

Kate wanted to accompany him on these visits, initially taking a couple of hours but more recently requiring the entire day. Bob was also acutely aware of the strains, not only on himself, but on her and therefore, when learning Jo was to be returning to Vancouver for the Olympics, suggested it was perhaps the right time to curtail his life.

No emails or text were sent after the women's agreement in Las Vegas to assist Kate. Having obtained the support of her friends, Kate requested the only communication be in person or by telephone, and only the times and logistics be conveyed electronically. Bob, also, in his usual methodological way, researched his own demise, deciding he simply required a bottle of good malt whiskey to be consumed, with the four women at his bedside. This would be followed by an excessive dose of his prescribed medication, enough to create a deep sleep, but not to cause suspicion, and then the four of them were to place his head in two plastic bags and tie them tight around his neck until his breathing stopped. It all seemed quite simple and according to numerous web sites visited in the Vancouver Public Library (so as not to arouse suspicion should their computers be searched later), completed within a few hours.

The chosen date and time was the evening of Friday February 12th, 2010, the day of the Vancouver Olympics opening ceremonies, when two thousand six hundred athletes from eighty-two nations would be welcomed into the arena. This was the time the police services would be most stretched, and when there would be few officers assigned to non-Olympic matters. There would be no interest in the death of a terminally ill man. The location of Bob and Kate's townhouse, close to the centre of town, meant the streets would be busy. The celebrations were scheduled to begin at six p.m. Bob decided this should also be the time he would start the process to end his life. During the preceding weeks, he was careful to make no hint to any of his friends or colleagues — he had no remaining family — that he was planning to take his own life, and was not going to let the disease run its full course. Many friends, when learning he had ALS, spoke of the scientist Stephen Hawking, who survived for decades with the diagnosis, suggesting that Bob should have faith that it could be the same for him. But Bob was sensible. He had read the reports and the research, been to the numerous self-help web sites, and spoken at length to empathetic hospice nurses and glassy-eyed doctors. He was a practical man, and while acutely aware he had been dealt a very raw deal, at a relatively young age, he knew there was nothing he could do except exit the world on his own terms, with dignity, and with the women he loved at his side, supported and loved by others who would be there for Kate when he was gone.

In this respect, Bob was deeply indebted to Jo, Andrea and Daphne. He recognised that men, no matter who they are, could never understand the full depth and strength of female friendship. During his life and varied careers, he had been fortunate to have a number of male friends, but remained aware that the friendship he experienced with these individuals — even Paul, his closest friend, known for over thirty years — was not as deep, nor as comprehensive, as the ones Kate had with hers.

While there were few secrets between Kate and Bob, when she returned from one of her 'girlfriend retreats', he found himself jealous of the conversations she enthusiastically recounted. The subject matter seemed to follow no order, nor knew no boundaries. No topic was off limits. Conversations on the quality and variety of vibrators (Japanese are the best), water purification, cures for muscle cramps, mothers, Vietnam, sushi, declining sex drives, the role of orgasms in stimulating brain cells, electric cars, Greenland, the French Revolution, growing tomatoes, Netflix and shoe insoles were all undertaken with the same passion and questionable knowledge by these four women. Opinions were challenged and frequently laughed at, but always listened to. He loved the rare occasions when he could be a fly on their wall. He was almost embarrassed to admit that when they arranged to meet in Vancouver, he actively encouraged Kate to host at their house, and then would attempt not to go out or be excluded so he could listen in, and maybe be invited to contribute to these gatherings. When he did leave, he returned to find four drunken women, empty wine bottles strung across the floor, giggling, speaking at the same time, yet in some unexplained way, able to hold and respond to all subject matter introduced. Their relationship was to be envied, and he did.

If he was fortunate enough to be party to these intimate late-hour gatherings, the women often became oblivious to his presence. With their guards down, he obtained an insight into the intricacies of the women's minds, and an additional comprehension of his wife.

Some men, he knew, found these female interactions tiresome and petty, but for Bob the emotion they promoted was envy. He was jealous that women had such a close bond; jealous he did not have a similar group of male friends he could share everything with; jealous that Kate had a relationship with three women, seemingly closer than the one she had with him. Consequently, when he thought about Kate existing in a world without him, he did so without considerable concern. Yes, she would miss him; yes, it would be extremely difficult; yes, she would feel considerable pain, but she had her friends. She would be looked after. She would be all right.

Jo arrived five days before the opening ceremony and although invited to stay with Andrea, she knew her place was small and she never really felt comfortable with Peter, nor knew him well, so politely declined. Daphne also offered her a bed but she recognised the deep tensions in Daphne's relationship, so although Daphne's place was huge, she told everyone she wanted her own space, and it was a business expense covered by her employer, so she would stay in a hotel. Jo booked a room in the Marriott overlooking the harbour. A few days before she was due to arrive, Kate called, asking her to stay with her. With Bob now downstairs there was ample room, and Jo's coming and going would ease the tense environment in the townhouse as the couple navigated their last few days together. Kate never acknowledged she needed Jo's presence to give her support, but it was tacitly recognised by both women. In travelling, Jo was used to her own space: at the end of a long day, full of negotiations, meetings and other people, she really appreciated it. But she also knew her friend needed her to provide a distraction to the planned events. She would keep the room at the Marriott as a bolthole but live at Kate's.

Kate had been given assurances that if she needed compassionate leave, it would be forthcoming. The Human Resources department of the RCMP were aware of her domestic situation, and at the outset appointed a woman called Maureen to act as a link between the organisation and the couple. Kate called Maureen on a couple of occasions, primarily concerning pensions and wages issues. She did not require her for the emotional or psychological support the organisation offered. She knew, when Bob was gone, that she would need to throw herself into her work as an escape from the huge void that would open, and Maureen would understand and facilitate this. Jo, Daphne and Andrea were there for all her emotional needs.

As the prearranged date grew nearer, Kate found life taking an unanticipated direction. Day-to-day activities were becoming increasingly problematic to complete. It was not just that she found it difficult to concentrate in meetings, or to hold a conversation with colleagues, but remembering where she had left her glasses, whether she had washed her hair when exiting the shower, what she wanted to eat for lunch, were all challenging thoughts. Often, when driving, she found she had forgotten her destination, having to stop the car and *think* where she was supposed to be going. Driving on the roads near to her home was also difficult: as the Games drew nearer, more restrictions were placed on the road network to accommodate the dignitaries, athletes and security services. Certain routes had been designated 'Olympic roads', meaning access was denied to the masses and lengthy alternatives were required. The media boasted that over five thousand volunteers were to be assisting with the Games, all having been given sky-blue rainproof jackets with logos; jackets worn by Vancouver residents for years after the Olympics had finished. Frequently, it seemed there were more of these individuals than residents or visitors in the city. It was a special time. Vancouver changed to 'Welcome the world', and while everyone in the city seemed to be on the same page, Kate was experiencing a detachment difficult to rationalise.

This detachment was most acutely felt when experiencing mundane everyday tasks, like buying a coffee from a barista at Starbucks and being asked, 'How is your day going?' and her response, 'Fine', when really the truth would be, 'I am preoccupied with thinking about my husband who I am about to help to die in five days.'

Similar questions, Kate mused, were asked millions of times a day and lies ensued, but generally these lies covered minor events. Someone would be unhappy because they broke a favourite mug, spilt nail polish on the carpet, forgot a friend's birthday, gained five pounds in weight in a week. Little things. But on rare occasions in one's life, these questions were asked following more significant events: learning that parents are divorcing; a close friend has been arrested for dealing drugs; employment has suddenly been terminated; the man you love is terminally ill. On these occasions, when someone asks how you are, you smile and lie. Similar lies also occur when happier events are taking place.

Many years previously, Kate had an affair with a colleague she first encountered when starting her three-month training at the RCMP training school in Regina. They met in the early 1980s and remained friends. A few years later, they found they were both working in the same town and, despite the knowledge that he was married, started sleeping together. She believed it not to be an affair: affairs presuppose some sort of deep affection and commitment. This was sex with a friend; justified as neither party wanted to take it further. Their infrequent liaisons involved a brief journey on public transport to a hotel on the outskirts of town, an alcoholic lunch (Kate maintained this was primarily a friendship and wanted to reconfirm to herself she did actually like this man before taking off her clothes), sex, conversations, a lot of humour, more sex, showers, goodbyes and the return journey. On travelling to these special encounters, she never read, nor listened to music, nor tried to work. She looked at her fellow travellers, trying to envisage if their journeys held as much excitement and anticipation as hers. She sat and glowed, wanting to somehow telepathically convey to one of them that she was about to enter a hotel to have sex for the afternoon. She would have liked to tell someone, to boast; to say, 'I'm going to a hotel for intimacy with a nice, married man, and afterwards we will return to our normal, mundane lives, and no one will know. Are you jealous?' but never did.

On one occasion the return journey was delayed, and she found herself talking to a woman in her seventies, about to babysit her two grandchildren. This was the only time Kate ever came close to divulging her secret. The woman wore a green, knitted hat. She remembered nothing else about her. What surprised Kate was the woman seemed unconcerned she was to be late for her commitment to her grandchildren. She was totally laid back and relaxed; not at all like other women in their seventies Kate had met. The sort of woman who would have been non-judgemental of the illicit rendezvous. When this woman asked Kate how her day was going, she was tempted to tell her of the liaison, of her justification, excitement, expectations, and see the stranger's reaction; to go into details, shared with no one, with a supportive stranger. But she did not. She lied, saying she was returning from meeting her sister for lunch. Ironically, this was the last journey to the hotel as soon afterwards, her lover received a promotion and moved to Ottawa. Over the years, their paths occasionally crossed, and on a couple of occasions he hinted they could start again, but with Bob she felt no need for intimacy with anyone else. Bob was her best friend and her best lover. No matter how easy, nor how flattering it would have been, there was no desire. And, if she was completely honest, the thought of taking off her clothes in front of a man who had last seen her naked in her twenties conjured up the same dread as sitting in the dentist's chair.

Kate had not told her girlfriends of this relationship, nor Bob, as he was acquainted with the man involved. It was her only secret. But now there was about to be another secret — far more serious. On the morning of February 12th 2010, when the Starbucks employee asked, 'Anything exciting on the agenda today?' she would not respond, "I am going to help my spouse to die'. She would lie and say, 'Nothing much. Watch the opening ceremonies like everyone else, I expect.'

Jo arrived at Kate's house around nine p.m. on the Monday prior to the opening ceremonies, dragging a huge suitcase, a little worse for wear following a day of intense sales meetings with the North American sales force of Holden Sealants. Eight men and two women, including Jo, comprised this group, who — over the next four weeks — would be tasked with promoting the name of Holden Sealants and the Vancouver Olympics. Each had been given the locations of the strategically placed advertisements, invites to sponsored events, and had new corporate attire comprising a bright yellow jacket and woollen hat with large pompom, complete with instructions to wear them at all times. The rain jackets were over-sized and a far cry from chic, and would not be worn following the Games, but certainly attracted attention. In wearing this apparel Jo felt they were like their own Olympic competing country, with more representation than some of the smaller African nations competing, and obviously more money to spend. The strict rules of marketing during the Games, and using the Olympic brand and logo, meant Jo and her colleagues had to tread a careful path to ensure they did not invoke the wrath of the huge legal team of the International Olympic Committee. In working with The Building Box, this was covered.

Jo was busy and preoccupied, conscious she needed to remain in this state and not dwell on what was to take place later in the week. While totally supportive of Bob and her best friend, she was acutely aware that the act they were to commit was illegal. When asked why she would be absent from the opening ceremonies, Jo fabricated an excuse concerning panic attacks when finding herself enclosed with large groups of people and prevented from easily leaving: she consequently felt unable to accept the much-coveted invitation. Upon giving her reasons, she felt immediately aware of her colleagues' doubts, but also knew there would be no challenge. As international sales director with a stellar resumé for advancing the reputation of the company, and in no small part responsible for their considerable annual sales bonuses, their respect was assured. Whatever her irrational reasons for missing this prestigious event, they would not be questioned.

Kate was expecting Jo's arrival. Bob was in bed in the former study. A hospital bed and walking frame had been delivered and installed by the ALS support group. The room, although now a little cramped, had a comfortable feel. The walls were covered with bookshelves; there was a couch and glass doors leading to a small patio. Bob was lying down: his large, six-foot frame had grown thin and wiry, grey stubble on his face. He was wearing sweatpants and a faded t-shirt with the logo of the 2005 Seattle half-marathon; a sad reminder of a former life. A blanket, which had become part of his permanent attire, was draped around his shoulders, causing Kate to give him the nickname Lionel, after the Peanuts cartoon character who always carried a blanket with him.

Jo clumsily deposited her case in the hallway, silently embraced Kate and headed straight to the study. The last time she had seen Bob, he was a happy, confident, fit individual with a full head of salt-and-pepper hair and wonderful blue eyes, rimmed with thick dark lashes; the result of eye drops he took to address glaucoma. Now it seemed as if only the eyes remained. Jo knew little about ALS, also known as Lou Gherig's disease in North America, after the famous baseball player who contracted it and died in 1941. This elite sportsman, known as the 'Iron Horse', was diagnosed with the illness at the young age of thirty-six and ended his career with an emotional address at the Yankee Stadium which is, even today, regarded as one of the best ever given by a sportsman. The speech was called 'The Luckiest Man on the Face of the Earth', in which Gherig stated that, despite being given a 'bad break', he had been lucky to do what he loved.

Known as motor neurone disease in Britain, or ALS (amyotrophic lateral sclerosis) in North America, Jo's knowledge had been gleaned from what Kate initially conveyed and from others, who, once she told them she had a good friend with ALS, recounted experiences they had with friends and acquaintances who were also victims. Those diagnosed start with the simple symptoms of feeling tired and run down; they have muscle pain and find it difficult to walk. These symptoms gradually increase. There is no cure. No one diagnosed has ever fully recovered. There are very few treatments to improve the quality of life. ALS does not affect the mind, only the body. One of the comments Jo read, which stayed with her, described it as 'the most amazing and most terrible of all diseases'. Once diagnosed, victims die — typically — within three years. It strikes both men and women, occurring at any age, but mostly diagnosed in middle age. No one knows why. The body gets tired and wastes away while the mind stays active. Swallowing becomes increasingly difficult, eating and drinking painful. It is a cruel, slow, painful way to die.

When Kate first told her friends of Bob's diagnosis, Jo visited numerous web sites to gain an understanding to support her friend. It was difficult to believe that was only ten months ago. Without exception, this information stressed the emotional toll not only for the patient, but for those tasked with looking after them. In embracing Kate and seeing Bob in bed, entering the room with the walking frame, sticks and bottles of pills, and smelling the space, she wondered how her capable friend was surviving. She questioned how she would cope if she received a similar diagnosis — who would care for her? — and deliberated whether she was strong enough to support her friend over the coming days.

Bob's eyes flickered upon hearing Jo enter his space, a smile came to his face and he attempted to sit up, but the effort was too great.

'So wonderful to see you, Jo,' he said in a husky voice she did not recognise. Sitting down on the bed, she took his hand while Kate appeared with a large glass of wine.

'You look like shit,' Jo said, adding, 'No wonder your wife doesn't want to sleep with you.' Bob started to laugh, but the action soon developed into an abrasive cough that all could see was painful. It lasted what seemed, to Jo, like an awfully long time, and when it stopped, Bob said, 'I am so ready to go; so ready to end this. I cannot thank you enough for what you and the other musketeers are about to do.' Jo looked at Kate, she expected to view some raw emotion but instead witnessed a compassionate woman totally at one with her husband's wishes. At that point, any doubts Jo was harbouring over the planned events of the next few days disappeared. This was the right decision, even if the entire Canadian Parliament and legal system believed it was not.

Jo's time in Vancouver was to be taken up with Holden Sealants work until the opening ceremonies. After this, she had booked a two-week vacation to remain and support her friend, but agreed to be on call for her employer, should they need her. Kate had not protested this decision. Although the ties between the four friends was uniform, if asked to name their best friend, Jo and Kate would have no hesitation selecting each other.

Years later, reflecting on this time, what surprised Kate most was how unemotional she felt. The termination of a life had been discussed, researched, rationally planned, executed in a way to cause least pain to everyone involved. The illegal killing, and it was just that, of a human being was conducted against the backdrop of intense celebrations, wild colours, games, competitions, singing, dancing, performances and parties. Olympic mascots strolled the various streets, which were full of young, fit athletes, residents, volunteers, visitors and the world's media. Over six hundred and fifty thousand visitors descended on

Vancouver during the two-week period. No one was sad. No one could imagine four women in a townhouse, only a short distance away from the lavish opening ceremonies for the 2010 Winter Olympics, were busy assisting a man they loved to die. The events were at opposite ends of the happiness spectrum.

The Olympics, by their very nature, celebrate the human body and the lengths this can be tested and challenged, what it can endure, the speeds it can achieve, the weight it can carry, the heights it can jump, how perfectly it can function alone or in unison with others. A terminal illness, such as ALS, painfully illustrates how easily and rapidly this body can fail; how fallible it is. How it need only be a matter of months before it is reduced to an empty vessel; to suddenly, without warning, break beyond repair, to become totally useless. No one wants to be exposed to this cruel fact.

The television coverage of the opening ceremonies began at three p.m. on 12th February. A large, flatscreen television covered one of the walls in Bob's room, displaying the arrival of dignitaries and showcasing the Olympic venues. The perpetual discussion, dominating since the Games were awarded, concerned whether there would be sufficient snow to stage some events. No doubt, it would be resurrected during this coverage. Daphne and Andrea arrived after lunch and were crowded around the bed. Daphne had a glass of wine, and the others drank tea. Bob had been poured a large glass of whisky, which he was sipping slowly but consistently. A third of the bottle, opened a few hours earlier, was gone. This was the only thing he had been able to consume. The disease made swallowing very painful, and consequently it became easier not to attempt to eat. While there had been discussions over a final meal, Kate knew this was not an option.

There had never been a time in the women's relationship when the conversation did not flow, and despite the circumstances of the day, this was again the case. Kate had been encouraged to find photographs of the group, which were few and far between in the early years before their fortieth birthdays' gathering in New York, and the advent of mobile telephones. Few images existed from the 1980s, when they all had large hairstyles and even larger shoulder pads. The few fuzzy photographs Kate found showed weddings, birthdays and children. The quantity increased as the years passed. Kate was fastidious in printing out images documenting key events in her, and Bob's, life. Photographs of her twenty-five years with him had been placed and meticulously labelled in albums, along with invites to parties, entrance tickets to museums and art galleries in foreign countries, exotic bus and rail tickets, and hotel and restaurant receipts. Each album, some of which — it seemed — had not been opened for years, beautifully catalogued a shared life. While the women pored over the documents, looking at images of holidays in Italy, Thailand, Japan, Germany, England and Australia, as well as numerous camping trips in North America, Jo could not help letting her mind wander to question who would want all these keepsakes after Kate was gone.

In past generations, there was nothing to preserve. Kate kept at least twenty photograph albums, and Jo knew that, while her own memorabilia did not mirror Kate's in quantity, nor in its systematic ordering, it did haphazardly exist in numerous cardboard boxes in her garage. Like Kate, there was no one to leave it to. No one would want it. Despite being married (whatever that meant), she was more alone than many women who had never entered this union. She had a cheating spouse she did not love, who, if she chose to leave, would be able to access the wealth she worked extremely hard for and earned over the last twenty years. Not for the first time, she fantasised over David suffering a similar fate to Bob. If this were the case, would she be there for him until the end? Would there be compassion and tears when that end came?

It was already dark outside and the television was featuring the rich and famous arriving at BC Place for the opening ceremonies. The commentators informed everyone that sixty-one thousand, six hundred people were in attendance and there were over four thousand, five hundred performers, all 'With Glowing Hearts' — the motto of the Vancouver Games. Daphne wondered, aloud, at the washroom capacity for that crowd as she heard that in New York City, on New Year's Eve, those on Times Square had to wear adult diapers because there were too few washrooms and too many people. A tray of sushi in the kitchen remained largely untouched, unlike the bottles of Pinot Gris being consumed at a pace. Kate replaced the albums on the bookshelves and Bob was encouraged to take more sips of whisky. He was drifting in and out of consciousness, seeming not to be listening to the conversations.

Jo, Daphne and Andrea were on the sofa looking at the screen, commenting on the attendees' clothes and the physical stature of the athletes, the volume having been increased slightly. Kate flitted between the various rooms with little obvious direction. No actual time had been chosen: 'the calm before the calm', thought Jo, as the opening ceremonies formally started with a tribute to a Georgian luge athlete, killed earlier in the day during a training session. This announcement prompted conversations over the tragedy of the event, the arrival at the apex of a career only to be denied by the cruel hand of fate. Before the discussion could be advanced, the doorbell rang, and the group were reminded of an outside world which had, for the last few hours, slipped from consciousness. Kate jested that she was expecting no one and moved out of the room. Animated female voices were subsequently heard, and Kate reappeared with a woman she introduced as Susan, one of the nurses assigned to care for Bob. This visit was unscheduled and it was explained that Susan had been attending another patient nearby, and that the visit had taken longer than anticipated. Upon returning to her car, she found it had been towed and with all the chaos, she decided to visit Bob before addressing the best way to retrieve her vehicle.

With the presence of someone frequently tasked with taking charge, Susan confidently entered their environment, introduced herself, and passing no judgement on the empty wine bottles in the room, nor the sheepish looks of those present, exited to wash her hands, returning as the opening ceremonies were starting. She looked at Bob, who remained asleep, and at the bottle of alcohol next to him, surrounded by containers of pills. For a split second her expression changed, then she collected herself, and with a sixth sense seemed to grasp the situation and what was planned. Through specialising in treating the terminally ill, and with particular empathy for victims of ALS, who — for some reason — always seemed such kind, sensitive souls, she held strong suspicions regarding why these women were assembled.

The group was also cognisant that Susan suspected their reasons for gathering around this man, and fidgeted on the sofa, exchanging furtive glances like guilty school children found smoking during recess when the headmistress arrives, unannounced. The ambiance in the room had altered in the presence of an outsider, but this was not a negative development. The euthanasia cloud was consistently present, as it undoubtedly is among so many rooms inhabited by the terminally ill. Susan's arrival had not blown it away.

The television brightly flickered. Bob remained asleep. Susan picked up the bottle of alcohol, studied the label and replaced it. She seated herself on the bed, bending down to speak to her patient, her face almost touching his. Bob's eyes opened and a smile passed his lips. He then whispered to her, quietly, so the others could not hear, 'I think it's time, don't you?' and closed his eyes. Within seconds, it seemed he was asleep again. Susan stood and addressed Kate directly, ignoring the others who were making poor attempts to focus on the screen, rather than the events in the room.

'Would you like me to give him something to help him sleep? The whisky has done quite a good job, but if you want him to have a really, really good sleep, I can give him some assistance.'

Kate nodded, as tears filled her eyes and those of her best friends. Susan reached for her bag, which looked more like a designer purse than a medical case, took out a vial and syringe and with no emotion delivered an injection. She moved away from Bob, instructing Kate to go and sit by him and take his hand. Picking up her bag, she glanced at the four women, immediately recognising the deep bond and love they all obviously shared. She shared a similar bond with her sister, and her best friend, and was thankful to exit this space knowing each woman was supported by another. So often, in the course of her work, she left an individual to grieve alone with no one to comfort them.

Susan did not consider what she had done was in any way wrong. She had the ability and mechanisms to terminate a life which, to all intents and purposes, was ended and she could do this without there being any pain, fulfilling the wishes of all involved. But she was also aware there were others who did not share these views. Turning to Kate, she addressed her directly.

'As this is an unscheduled visit, you may not want to mention it to anyone, but I will call you tomorrow morning to check on you and Bob.' Kate nodded while Jo got up to show Susan out.

After Susan had gone, the four women sat in silence. Nelly Furtado and Brian Adams were singing on the stage as the crowd applauded and sang along. As Bob slowly fell into a deeper, peaceful sleep, the cameras panned the audience and athletes. An illuminated spirit bear appeared on the stage. Less than a mile from the start of the 2010 Winter Olympic Games, a man slowly slipped away and peacefully died.

'I expected to feel something else. Some huge emotion, something to happen to me, but I didn't,' Kate said. The others all spoke at once and then stopped. They looked at Bob and cried in silence.

Daphne and Andrea left a couple of hours later. Kate telephoned the on-call doctor, who arrived in the early hours of the morning and arranged for the removal of the body. No questions were asked, as the doctor expressed no surprise at the course of events. Instead, in his matter-of-fact manner, he explained that ALS can be quite unpredictable and if there is no fight, many patients die earlier than expected. The doctor provided Kate with a form entitled 'Expected Death at Home' which enabled her to contact the funeral director immediately. While euthanasia remained a crime in Canada, it soon became apparent, to both Kate and Jo, that concerns they had about undertaking this deviant act were completely ill founded. It was occurring frequently, and like so many deviant acts, such as homosexuality or the use of cannabis — which society deemed crimes in the past, only to decriminalise at a later date — all knew it would only be a matter of time before those who were terminally ill and wanting to die could do so with dignity, on their own terms.

Over the course of the following two weeks, while the City of Vancouver and the world retained their preoccupation with the competitions and the medal table, and the manufacture of snow — requiring transportation from another mountainous area, over two hundred and fifty kilometres away — Jo and Kate built on their already strong relationship. Kate methodically removed Bob's clothes and personal possessions from their home; cleared the kitchen cabinets of the food and spices only he ate; dispensed of the male cosmetics in the bathroom; sold his bike and car; and gave all his tools — and the items, the functions of which she could not determine — to his best friend Paul. Jo was impressed with the orderly detachment with which this was done, but Kate explained it had not been unexpected: she had time to mentally prepare. She had lost her shared life with Bob months ago and accepted it was time to move on. In many respects she was glad to put an end to this chapter; to the daily unannounced arrival of nurses and doctors, visits to the hospital, well-meaning friends dropping by and the vast assortment of medical equipment taking up space in her abode. She explained that, after the death, she found it almost a relief not to be totally consumed thinking about their imminent destiny. She could, at last, take a breath and examine her life and see the world in a new way.

As Jo watched the transition of the neat, trendy townhouse to *Kate's* neat, trendy townhouse, she found herself becoming jealous. Kate was now her own person: totally independent, consulting no one, all decisions her own. Not for the first time did Jo dream of a life without David, the man who denied her offspring; the man who was continuing to sleep with other women; the man who was using her.

The night before Jo was due to return to England, the four women met at a small wine bar. The evening started early, at four p.m. To avoid the crowds, a discrete location in the suburbs with circular booths, subtle lighting and a mature clientele was selected, conducive to the women's final night together. Though still raw, it was uniformly agreed that Kate was doing well: she had lost weight, changed her hairstyle, added highlights and proudly announced the purchase of a new car. Due to start work the following week, she had already been answering a few phone calls and responding to emails. A few days previously, she was asked to be part of the team accompanying the Canadian contingent of Olympic athletes and dignitaries to the next Summer Olympics in London, England in July 2012. With Jo residing in the outskirts of London, the topic of conversation centred on the logistics of this and for them all to meet again across the Atlantic, the time that could be taken, and whether it was feasible to explore other European cities, such as Paris or Amsterdam, as well as London, when they met.

This meeting was to be the last time the four would get together for some time, and there was an urgency they all felt to address important topics. Kate was conscious that the focus was on her and felt keen to move the topic on to one they could all equally contribute to. She chose the subject of the mid-life crisis and the menopause, aware — after spending an intense period with Jo — that Jo was experiencing symptoms. She suspected these to be severe, but Jo had not fully opened up. Kate wanted to give her the opportunity to share.

About the time Bob received his diagnosis, Kate started to experience the clichéd symptom of the menopause — hot flushes. Although mentioned by Kate as a ploy to distract attention from herself, as Kate expected, Jo leaped enthusiastically on the subject matter, which of course held a similar level of interest to the others. It was agreed that, in contrast to puberty, where prepubescent girls receive hours of detailed classroom instruction at elementary and middle school concerning its onset, changes in the body, periods, hormonal imbalances, sex and contraception, no such in-depth tuition is available for women of their age approaching menopause, which was just as life-altering as puberty.

All agreed that the menopause was primarily the subject of jokes. The understanding that these four university-educated women had of the profound changes beginning to take place in their bodies was based on a few articles read in the magazines in dentist or hair-stylists' waiting rooms. This, all confirmed, was pitiful. They were all having periods, but Daphne and Andrea said their cycles were now lighter and shorter; Jo never knew when she would bleed, nor for how long; and Kate sometimes went months without buying tampons. The group uniformly spoke of increasing difficulty sleeping over the last few years. Daphne said she heard sex drive decreases with age, and all nodded at this, then laughed. Was it age, or the fact they had the same partner for so long? Is it physical or psychological or both, they asked each other, providing no intimate details, nor definitive conclusion. While the topic had quickly taken a more light-hearted direction, Jo was keen not to distract from its importance, adding that in addition to hot flushes, she was getting more agitated, with mood swings and frequently an obsession over matters she exaggerated out of all proportion. She felt the menopause was far more devastating than she ever thought and went on to give a full account of her health and hormones, as the others, intent on gaining any knowledge they could, listened intently. Jo had obviously conducted the most homework and wanted to share, coming as little surprise to Kate.

Jo explained that, initially, she tried to deny it was happening and that her body was changing and getting older. Quite soon after turning fifty, she started to experience hot flushes, huge surges of heat across her head and torso, sweats, 'glows' and considerable discomfort, totalling as many as twenty a day. They started the moment she got out of bed, gaining in strength and length after she took her first cup of beloved coffee, and then occurring without warning throughout the day and night. There seemed to be little order or rationale, but were induced with coffee and spicy food. The others listened without interruption. With an attentive audience, Jo explained she was frequently awakened during the night, covered in a sweat as her body experienced the surge of heat, lasting only a couple of minutes and that she often went to sleep immediately afterwards, lying in damp sheets.

Jo went on to describe the day that changed her life. While at her gym, she saw an advertisement from researchers at the local university, who were studying hot flushes. The poster stated, 'Do You Suffer from Severe Hot Flushes (more than eight) a Day?' She had suddenly realised that, in experiencing over twenty, her condition was acute. She was indeed on the extreme end of the menopausal hot-flush scale and needed help. Kate looked at her friend, who seemed to be getting passionate, talking quickly in an emotionally charged state, looking as if she was about to cry. Reaching out, she touched her arm. 'Why did you not tell us?' Kate asked. Jo sighed, saying she believed this was normal and was maybe overreacting, but now realised she was not.

Kate, Daphne and Andrea exchanged concerned glances, never before having witnessed such an ardent vocalisation on any subject from Jo, who was normally the most rational and sensible of the group. All were unsure whether it was better to let her continue or curtail the conversation and change the topic to something more light hearted and less distressing.

Demonstrating no desire to stop, Jo went on to explain of other, more subtle changes to her body; ones she had not attributed to a hormonal change but upon reflection, probably were. Despite regular exercise, she found it easy to gain weight and her skin's elasticity was changing. She had developed what the English refer to as 'bingo arms' — layers of flabby skin at the top of the underarm which, no matter how many weights lifted, planks sustained or press-ups achieved, never appeared to abate. Her breasts, once pert, firm and attractive, now sagged and when she jumped up and down bits of flab around her body bounced. But the most shocking development of excess flab was on her pubic mound; an area she thought would be immune to weight gain. This, too, developed spare skin, easily pinched. To add insult to injury, there were grey hairs, completing the area's total lack of attraction. Although deadly serious, at this point Kate, Daphne and Andrea were having problems containing their laughter. The waitress passed and quipped, 'Having a good time, ladies?'

Jo had clearly not finished, wanting to continue her tirade by going on to explain it was not just physical changes she was noticing. Daphne shook her head, took a large gulp of wine and between muffled giggles from Andrea and Kate, injected that she thought this tragic story could not get any worse, questioning whether it really was something they should be spending their time on in these final few precious hours together. But Kate and Andrea encouraged Jo to elaborate, enjoying the way the topic had now taken a more entertaining and humorous turn. Daphne fell back in her chair, careful not to let the wine glass spill any of its contents, and despite wanting to pursue other conversations, acquiesced to the dominant demands of the group.

All were more than a little drunk, and while the alcohol made Andrea and Daphne giggly and Kate smiley, Jo remained committed, emotional and passionate in her delivery. She wanted them to fully appreciate how important an understanding of the menopause was. It was increasingly a component of who she was, and her best friends needed to be made aware of this. She went on to stress that even more alarmingly than these physical changes they found comical, were the cognitive ones, which certainly were not.

On numerous occasions, Jo found it impossible to recall someone's name, the word she needed for a description, a town's location, what programme she watched on television the night before, even really simple things, like the name of the child actor who starred in The Wizard of Oz, were beyond her capacity. Her career demanded the delivery of numerous presentations, previously conducted with confidence and without difficulty. Unlike many of her colleagues, she liked being in front of a crowd with well-prepared overheads and an attentive audience. Recently, she wondered if she was 'losing it' as these presentations had not gone well, as she lost her train of thought. Afterwards, colleagues were asking if she felt all right. On a couple of occasions, her mind had drawn a complete blank and there followed awkward silences and fidgeting in the room. At first, she attributed these failings to the stresses of the job, but upon deeper analysis started to wonder if there was a connection between hormonal mid-life changes and her new being.

Her friends had now stopped laughing and were uncharacteristically quiet. Knowing she had spoken at length, Jo abruptly finished her domination of the conversation. She could see Andrea had a glazed look, Kate an alcohol-induced indifference and Daphne was failing in her attempt to disguise boredom. Jo also recognised that if she spoke any more, she would cry. It was not the time to tell them that, after reading the research advertisement concerning the severity of hot flushes, she made an appointment to see her doctor, Carol, who she had known for many years, was of a similar age, and of their subsequent conversation and her commitment to Hormone Replacement Therapy (HRT). HRT was controversial and her friends may not be supportive of her decision and could try to persuade her this was not the right path to take. It was not the time to speak of it.

There was an awkward silence, then Daphne quickly succeeded in changing the subject to their next meeting in London. Feeling emotional and fragile, Jo had no appetite to join in. She started to reflect on her relationship with her doctor, Carol, and how it had radically changed her life. Making the excuse she needed to make a telephone call to work, Jo took the phone from her purse, left the group, and thankfully headed outside to the cool, sobering evening air. She needed composure and time alone, knowing they would understand. There was a bench in front of the bar: sitting down, she reflected on her menopausal journey and her brilliant key influencer — Carol.

Carol was aware of Jo's career and stressful lifestyle, having been heavily involved with her unsuccessful journey to obtain fertility, and she was instrumental in referring her to the numerous specialists who knew more about the female reproductive system than she did. Following all the tests, Jo told her of their decision to not pursue the dream of children, telling her they just decided to move on, and after three years did not want to spend any more time, energy and money. At the time, Carol said she was being very sensible, as many of her patients became preoccupied with their desire to conceive and suffered immense emotional stress pursuing this dream. Much later, when Jo learned of David's deception, she did not tell Carol. There would have been no point.

In another world, Carol and Jo would have been close friends, but circumstances required they retained a professional doctor/patient link, reflective of the code of ethics Carol signed annually. At this appointment, the topic of HRT was introduced. Jo explained that her understanding was limited, based on information gleaned from magazines or reports on the radio over the years, and rarely paid attention to. The menopause happened to other women — a group of women Jo had nothing in common with: older women, another generation, existing in an arena she did not enter, and therefore of little interest. She did think there was a link between HRT and breast cancer and therefore should be avoided. She was looking for advice and a rapid end to the sweaty surges of body heat, and what she recognised as a very emotional, unpredictable state.

Carol's office contained a faded photograph of her three school-aged children on a beach with their father, and a poster showing crossroads and a signpost pointing in two different directions, with one direction stating, 'The road taken' and the other saying, 'No longer an option.' Jo had always been drawn to this image, and the idea that once a decision is made, there is no going back. These were the only personal items in this small consultation room. The bland cream-painted walls had framed certificates of Carol's medical qualifications, together with a noticeboard displaying irregularly placed internal diagrams of the eye, female reproductive organs, knee joint and chest. All looked as if they had been produced in the 1960s and not updated. There was a small stool on casters for the doctor to sit on, a chair and an examination couch. Jo had forgotten how many occasions she had been here, naked from the waist down, feet in stirrups, being asked to slide down the couch so her vagina was easily accessible for the investigative probing procedures a woman's preventative medicine demanded. Jo took these examinations in her stride, often surprised in the routine, detached way they were conducted. As another woman delved deep into her most intimate anatomical part, the weather, holidays, kids, television programs were discussed. Very occasionally she was asked if there was any pain. Neither party wanted to think too deeply about what was happening.

Carol told Jo to get undressed, and left the room. Jo removed her skirt and underwear, climbed on the couch and lay back. Alone, waiting for her doctor to return, she pondered on how the people invited to touch her vagina were so dissimilar and did so in such divergent ways. The medical profession explores the vagina by demanding legs be placed in stirrups. The patient lies flat on her back, staring at Styrofoam white ceiling tiles, noticing the stains and cobwebs. The doctor finds latex gloves to wear, liberally applies gel to explorative tools, and with the minimal of warning (the appointment should be undertaken in under ten minutes to avoid the patients backing up in the waiting room and the receptionist becoming annoyed), cold, metallic instruments are used to force the vagina apart, tissue is scraped, collected and placed into small, labelled, transparent test tubes. Deep vaginal probing conducted. When the task is successfully completed, abrasive paper towels are given to wipe the gel, and the experience, away.

In another world, lovers playfully and tenderly finger the vagina, while at the same time caressing other body parts. This may take some considerable time, lasting anything from seconds to hours, causing the necessary dilation. Did she not read somewhere, the vagina swells three times its size with mental and physical stimulation? Eyes frequently closed, all body parts utilised, but the objective, the goal, the medal, is the vagina. Gels are not obligatory as natural lubrication oozes. Sex toys are not cold nor metallic. The mind does not look at the ceiling tiles but focuses on the object of the act. Once achieved, soft tissues may be applied to address excess fluids. When was the last time her vagina had been touched in this way? 'Ready?' Carol said, entering the room, catapulting her patient back from her fantasy.

The examination was quickly over. Carol snapped off her gloves and put them into the sealed container designed for the purpose of clinically and hygienically removing these objects, averting her eyes from Jo who got down from the couch to retrieve her underwear, then Carol started to give her understanding of the Hormone Replacement Therapy debate.

Although there was some controversy about taking HRT, there were also considerable benefits in the prevention of osteoporosis. Carol explained HRT was first available in the 1940s, becoming more commonly prescribed in the 1960s, but a couple of reports linked it to cancer, promoting a huge backlash. She explained there was a generation of women effectively denied this drug, which she enthusiastically described as ground breaking and life changing. She thought there were benefits, not only for hot flushes but for many of the other symptoms associated with the hormonal changes, such as mood swings, memory loss, emotional imbalances, vaginal dryness, weight gain and declining sex drive; all traits Jo was experiencing. At this point, Jo was desperate for anything, so without hesitation requested HRT, and despite it being early days, had not regretted the decision. Hot flushes were now gone. Her emotional rollercoaster, while still in existence, had dissipated, and while there were still issues with her memory, she did not think these were so bad. She had no idea about her sex drive as it ceased years ago.

Sitting outside the bar, Jo recognised she felt a little shy and apprehensive conveying to her friends the need to turn to, and be so dependent on, what many deemed to be controversial drugs, to deal with her emotions. Currently, her hormonal imbalances and the hot flushes were in check. Everything was good, thanks to the HRT miracle medication. She planned to take it for a couple of years and then life would have moved on, she would be older and it would no longer be needed.

'Everything okay?' Kate asked, having arrived unannounced at Jo's side.

'Yes, just finished the call,' Jo lied, seeing her friend was aware of this invention, but would not challenge her. Kate understood her completely, so knew when not to push. The two women returned inside and to the group. With the subject of the menopause seemingly addressed, another bottle of wine had been ordered, and the women's conversation moved on to the elephant in the room — the assistance with a death.

'I just did not think anything we did was wrong,' said Andrea, nervously articulating what the others thought. Jo was the first to notice the tears silently rolling down Kate's cheeks and asked if the conversation was too much for her to bear.

Kate shook her head, replying, 'No, we have no secrets. We need to talk it out. It's important for us all to express to each other what we feel.'

'Well, I'm with Andrea,' said Daphne, reaching for the wine bottle and filling up all the glasses on the table.

The beauty of their friendship was the honesty with which everyone could be themselves. No acts were required, as is so often the case in female relationships which frequently indulge a large dose of competitiveness. No one was judgemental: they all mutually supported each other, trusted each other, respected one another. They recognised this shared secret only acted to facilitate the strengthening of this bond and their loyalty to each other.

There was no suspicion by the medical profession or the coroner that Bob's death was premeditated and not the result of a terminal illness. These four middle-aged women were guilty of assisting a suicide, but no one in authority cared. Bob's life and death had been recorded, the paperwork completed, his pain ended. It had, in retrospect, been easy. Any ethical considerations they may have had prior to the day of the opening ceremonies were unfounded. They were all in agreement. While the Vancouver Olympics provided a distraction, they concurred that even without this event to shield them, they would not have been detected.

The conversation moved on to Jo's departure to England the following day and their next planned meeting in the summer of 2012 in London. Daphne asked, in a casual way, about Jo's relationship with David. Feeling as if she had already dominated the conversation throughout the evening, and not having consumed quite enough wine to tell her best friends again of his continued affairs, his increasingly expensive tastes eroding her salary — which, last year was three times greater than his — his frequent long absences and their lack of communication, she unconvincingly said everything was fine and excused herself to head for the washroom. They all knew everything clearly was not.

Chapter 3
Inspire a Generation
London, Summer Olympics 2012

Jo sat on a stool in her large, designer kitchen at the island, laptop open in front of her, displaying a spreadsheet listing names and contact information, glass of wine adjacent. She adored her house and especially the kitchen. When taking the plunge to invest in London's real estate, she had spent almost a year looking at properties whenever time allowed. The search had been worth it. As work evolved, and travel commitments increased, having a home you loved to retreat to was priceless. The flatscreen TV was playing the film 'Sleepless in Seattle' without volume. She had seen it numerous times, but it still made her cry. Tom Hanks looked incredibly young, sharing an on-screen rapport with Meg Ryan rarely repeated in real life. True relationships were not like that.

It was eight thirty p.m. and Jo had spent the day in the offices of her long-term employer, Holden Sealants. The office was strategically located close to the country's key transportation routes; the M25 that circled the capital, the M1 serving the north, and Heathrow Airport. Founded twenty-five years ago by a down-to-earth Yorkshire man called Bernard Trim (who was anything but trim), this upstart sealant manufacturer had succeeded in challenging many of the established sealant companies, growing to be one of the largest in the world, with significant sales in Europe, North America and the East. It was now targeting the rapidly growing markets of South America. As the manager responsible for international sales, Jo worked a lot from home and travelled at least two weeks every month. For this inconvenience, which for the most part she enjoyed, she was very well rewarded. Her husband's employment also took him away, but only for a few days a month. The car-leasing company he worked for only served the United Kingdom, not warranting trips abroad.

She expected David to be home when she entered, but the house was empty, cold and silent, giving the impression he had not returned for days. With no children or lodgers or animals, it frequently reminded her of a real estate agent's 'show house': neat, tidy, with few articles suggesting anyone slept in the bedrooms or cooked in the kitchen. They never entertained. Friends and acquaintances tended to be related to work, and they socialised separately with colleagues after work, never during weekends. David had no close family, and Jo's were in the north, too old now to travel to see her. She visited them every Christmas for a few days. In the past, on rare occasions, David came but recently chose to be with his friends over her family, so she spent Christmas without him. Being an only child, Jo phoned her parents every Sunday, without exception, speaking primarily to her mother for about an hour, but always saving a few words specifically for her dad before terminating the contact. The small-town girl from a northern working-class town, who could frequently be found drinking Pinot Gris wine in her granite bespoke kitchen, needed this grounding on a regular basis. The phone calls provided that.

It was Wednesday night and her working week had so far consisted of trying to organise a boat cruise for one hundred and fifty people down the River Thames, the night before the London Olympic Games were to start, Thursday July 26th, 2012. Jo originally wanted the excursion to take place on the day of the opening ceremonies, but the security issues surrounding the rental of a pleasure cruiser at this time were immense, so plans had to be changed. In addition, some of the senior management at Holden Sealants had been invited to the New Olympic Stadium to see the opening ceremonies and were not willing to sacrifice one party for another. The most expensive tickets at this Olympic event were over two thousand pounds. The Holden Sealant river cruise could not compete with this star-studded cast, which included the Queen of England, Rowan Atkinson (Mr. Bean), Daniel Craig (James Bond) and Sir Paul McCartney.

Jo allocated herself twenty 'discretionary tickets' to the cruise, and while most had to be given to customers and potential customers, four had been put aside for

Kate, Daphne, Andrea and David. Her role at this event was primarily to introduce people to one another and network, not be the star of the show — this was to be Bernard's, the owner's, night. In tasking her to organise it, Bernard Trim was again acknowledging the exemplary way she dealt with colleagues and customers. These social skills are often a trait under-valued by traditional businesses, who demand employees work their way up the necessary promotional ladder before receiving increased status and promotion, but Jo's were recognised early in her career by Bernard and those at Holden, who knew she had attributes difficult to quantify. People liked her, and because of this they purchased sealant. To a traditional Yorkshire man who wanted value for his investments, it was not rocket science. It was thinking outside the corporate, traditional box, and worked very well for generating income.

The Holden Sealant's Cruise Organising Committee consisted of four junior sales colleagues, all chosen by Jo as they could work well together and to a deadline. They were liaising with the boat company's event planner — a hyperactive, attentive Asian man with an East London accent and in his late twenties, called Michael, who flamboyantly told her 'anything was possible.' Jo had to remind him that his client, on this occasion, was a very conservative sealant manufacturer, not a new trendy software company, so regrettably traditional and safe would have to be the order of the day. They decided on a simple buffet-food menu, a limited free bar consisting of wine, beer and soft drinks (but with a generous cash limit Bernard had agreed), a start time at seven thirty p.m., sailing at eight p.m. and a return time of eleven p.m. The cruise would travel to the Thames Barrier, sixteen kilometres downriver. The tides had been checked and were accommodating. There would be a dance floor and attire suggested as smart/casual, therefore covering everyone's preference. Michael organised caterers, and Jo signed contracts and arranged payments. He assured her he would be there every step of the way and was quick to return emails and telephone calls. Jo liked his persona and although a bit over energetic, he was obviously good at his job. And Michael liked dealing with Jo. Working with this well-organised woman was a lot easier than catering for a wedding reception often involving two competing families, or a twenty-first birthday function with a lot of under-age, obnoxious revellers.

With only a limited number of people allowed on the vessel, Jo and her team had to be selective. A considerable amount of time and negotiation was taken sorting names into 'gold', 'silver' and 'bronze' categories. The gold group received their invites first and had time to respond. Once numbers were known, the silver group received invites, and finally it was the turn of the bronze group.

Of course, there were also a number of the company's management team who wanted invites, as did their partners. Jo would have liked to invite more of the younger, enthusiastic sales team, who she knew would grease the wheels of the evening and add an age balance. While on the front line for gaining sales and securing the company's growth, these individuals were not far enough up the corporate totem pole to warrant a presence, and therefore had to be satisfied with any leftover buffet food which could be salvaged and returned to the office the following day.

Another huge problem the organising team had was gender balance, or rather imbalance. Despite it being the twenty-first century, Holden Sealants, not unlike other manufacturers of building products, was still comprised primarily of men, especially further up the hierarchy. At the numerous building conferences and trade shows, especially the more prestigious international ones in Cologne, Germany and in Las Vegas, Jo often found herself walking through a sea of dark suits. Certain professions attract men, others appeal to women, and without question the home improvement sector attracted the former. What young girl in her right mind, when asked where she would like to work when she graduated high school, would ever say 'for a company making sealant, or ladders, or paint, or spanners'? Female friends often expressed envy over Jo (and Kate's) male-dominated environments, but both women were quick to explain the men employed in their sectors were not the sort you wanted to date, let alone sleep with or build a life with. There were of course, exceptions, as Bob showed, but for the most part their male colleagues were professional to work with, yet that was where the bonding ended.

Jo studied the laptop full of names, deciding gender balance could be addressed tomorrow when she was more awake, and turned her attention to the television. Tom Hanks and Meg Ryan had finally met, his son was glowing at his father and potential new mother. Who would not want Meg Ryan as a mother? Slurping wine at the age of fifty-three, Jo calculated her desired child would be aged fifteen, if born in 1997, which was the year she stopped the infertility treatment, accepting a life without children. She fingered the stem of her glass. Since taking Hormone Replacement Therapy, she rarely cried, and never broke down in the way she did a few days every month when she was younger and menstruating. Her emotions were in check, constrained in the HRT drug noose, but the pain of being childless still ran deep, and recently the thoughts of what could have been were punctuating more of her waking hours. If anyone she trusted asked about the gaps in her life, there would be no hesitation in saying it was the lack of children. This is what she most regretted. No one's life is perfect: everyone has elements missing. We all look at others jealously and covet what is another's. But her gaps were not of her making: hers were the result of one man. David. And the gaps were widening as she got older.

It was starting to get dark outside. Jo realised she had not eaten and had to rise early tomorrow morning. The screen saver on her laptop showed an image of four, happy, slightly inebriated women during an evening in Las Vegas three years ago. She blew kisses back at her friends, closed the device, switched off the television and lights, re-checked the door and went to bed, leaving half a bottle of wine and glass on the counter.

Kate was the first of the group of friends to arrive in London, a week before the London Olympic Games were due to start, doing so with a group of twenty police colleagues on an Air Canada flight. In true bureaucratic style, each colleague was allocated a seat reflecting their rank and status. Kate was assigned 'Premium Economy', being in the middle of the status groups. The RCMP officers had been tasked with overseeing the security of the Canadian dignitaries in attendance, the athletes, and basically anyone deemed important who held a Canadian passport. It was well recognised to be a 'cushy number' as security was actually the responsibility of the host nation, and therefore the British Police were the de facto organisation who should be looking after the Canadians on British soil, and all other nations. The Canadian contingency did not want to step on the toes of their law-enforcement brothers and sisters, and had therefore been instructed to offer advice and support when asked to do so, but not upset any apple carts the hosts had in place.

Having been a serving police officer for over ten years, Kate knew the policing of Canadians was comparatively easy in comparison to the policing of nationals from other countries. The huge United States Olympic Games Security contingency presented the largest problem for the host nation, as not only did the US Law Enforcement Agencies want to check and double check every aspect of Britain's security, believing theirs to be superior, but they were tasked with protecting the most high-profile attendees. Michelle Obama — the wife of President Obama — presidential candidate Mitt Romney and Microsoft founder, Bill Gates, to name but three, all accepted invitations. The United Kingdom dignitaries not only comprised *all* the Royal Family, but the soccer star David Beckham, the Harry Potter author, JK Rowling, and performers Mick Jagger and Paul McCartney, as well as the mayor of London, Boris Johnson. The president of Russia, Vladimir Putin, was attending with a huge entourage to promote the forthcoming 2014 Sochi Winter Olympics, and no doubt to 'learn from the mistakes' of the London Games. The chancellor of Germany, Angela Merkel, and the president of France, Francois Hollande, were also due to attend.

Kate thought no one would know the names of the great and the good representing Canada. The Right Honourable David Johnston, the Governor General of

Canada, and Gordon Campbell, the High Commissioner for Canada, were not household names in Great Britain. For the most part, no one in Canada knew of them. Sometimes there were benefits from being from a country many thought of as 'bland'.

London was the first city to host the modern Olympics on three occasions: 1908, 1948 and 2012. The 2012 Summer Olympics was the biggest gathering of world leaders ever held in Britain. The media reported one hundred and twenty heads of state would be attending, with each leader accompanied by his/her own personal security detail. Civil servants in the UK Foreign Office had spent years developing a highly detailed and specific 'Dignitary Programme', specifically for the Games. This was a logistic nightmare for the civil servants working on databases and lists comprised months before the event. Carefully planned arrangements were frequently jettisoned when, at the last minute, a high-ranking dignitary suddenly decided to visit, having previously declined the invitation. Consequently, numerous British civil servants were looking tired and stressed.

The Canadian diplomats and civil servants at Canada House, home of the Canadian Embassy in London, had already been working with the British Foreign Office on the security issues for the Games. Kate's first meeting was in this lovely building, located in Trafalgar Square in central London. After introductions, and seated around a large, oval, polished, antique teak table, where tea and biscuits were served on china crockery, it was quickly agreed that the British had everything well organised and unless there was some absolute catastrophe, the Canadian security detail would show up, keep a low but supportive profile and not intrude. The Canadian diplomats produced a list (not extensive) of the high-profile Canadians attending and assured everyone that while a couple of guests did have a drinking problem, none had been flagged as causing embarrassment. Kate tried to remember the last time a Canadian caused any sort of embarrassment anywhere. She could not.

The British Foreign Office had prepared two dossiers for the Canadian security personnel. The first listed all the athletic events and their location. The second was significantly larger and catalogued the social events, the Canadians who were invited and the probability of their attendance. What was required at this meeting was for each of the attending Canadian security detail to select which of these champagne receptions, breakfast meetings, afternoon teas, evening parties, medal ceremonies and other miscellaneous functions they would attend. It was indeed going to be a hard couple of weeks. Kate immediately questioned whether she had packed enough clothes and whether her expenses would stretch to shopping in Knightsbridge to address the problem. Her male colleagues, she felt sure, were not preoccupied with the same thoughts. She scribbled a star against the closing ceremonies and focused on the early evening soirées having a designated finish time. She did not want to remain, long into the night, babysitting a crusty, retired, Canadian politician dining out on a reputation held decades ago. She had had enough experience of that earlier on in her career. There were a couple of appealing parties given by the French and the Italians. Experience informed her these were likely to be intimate affairs with good-looking men and excellent food and wine. She avoided those hosted by the Greeks, knowing they tended not to commence until after eleven p.m., or by the Brazilians, which would undoubtedly be loud, involve flamboyant dancing and not end until the early hours of the morning.

Kate sat back surveying the scene, not for the first-time marvelling at the sheer organisation involved in staging the Olympic Games. She felt honoured to have been awarded the opportunity to be part of this and to glean an understanding, of the Games that few saw. The media do an excellent job profiling the athletes, and the competitions, but give scant attention to those beavering away, for years, in the background. In deciding to hold the Olympics in the cash-strapped City of London, whose budget for the Games eventually reached US$15 billion (Beijing in 2008 was US$6.8 billion, whereas the 2014 Sochi Olympics was estimated to reach US$51 billion), the security issues were huge.

London had a long history of terrorist disruption. Memories of the horrific Islamic suicide attacks on public transport centres in July 2005, killing fifty-two people from eighteen nationalities and injuring over seven hundred, could never be forgotten. The budget in London, just for security, was originally set at £282 million (US$350 million) but increased to £553 million (US$700 million). Over ten thousand police offices and thirteen thousand, five hundred members of the armed forces were tasked to work on the event. While Londoners tended to take the ever-present terrorist threat in their stride, visitors, especially tourists, radically alter and cancel travel plans when bombs explode. Kate was only one of thousands of qualified individuals tasked to work at the fringes of the Olympics, for which security was their raison d'être. The security of the Games was extremely complex, eating up a large component of London's Olympic budget; a factor seriously considered by each city contemplating hosting the Games. It was the reason many cities give when deciding against holding them.

Following the long morning meeting, Canada House catered for a buffet lunch for their guests. Kate did not want to attend. This was her first full day in the capital and knowing the demands on her time during the next few weeks would be considerable, she needed to escape. Lunch was the only thing remaining on the day's agenda and an early exit meant she could take a slow walk, through Green Park and on to Knightsbridge, for shopping. She made her excuses, which no one seemed to mind, and headed out of the impressive building onto

Trafalgar Square. In the distance she could see the Countdown Clock, showing how many days, hours and minutes remained before the London Games started. It was warm but not hot. She stood for a moment, marvelling at the sheer volume of people moving in front of her. No matter how many times she visited London, this was always a surprise. Growing up in a small town on the Canadian Prairies could not prepare her for this force of people of every age, size and colour. London was wonderfully multicultural and exciting: staging the Olympic Games only made it more so.

Andrea and Daphne landed at London's Heathrow Airport on the Sunday morning, prior to the opening of the Games, following a crowded, nine-hour overnight flight from Vancouver. Although easily able to afford Business Class, Daphne knew this was not an option for Andrea, so slummed it in coach. It was the school holidays, so the number of children pacing the aisles and the level of noise was considerable. Although both women tried to sleep on the flight, neither succeeded.

Jo recommended they stay in a two-bedroomed apartment she knew of, which was part of a hotel complex in the vibrant Earls Court area of London. She frequently placed international business colleagues at this four-star establishment, which offered a variety of accommodation options from single bedrooms to three-bedroom suites with four-poster beds. It consisted of several Victorian houses blended together, offered a light breakfast, and was wonderfully close to the Piccadilly line underground station and restaurants, bars, and supermarkets, but unlike many other centrally located hotels, it was very quiet. The real bonus, however, was the direct underground tube line from Heathrow Airport to the establishment.

They checked into the hotel's two-bedroom suite just after one p.m. Like many visitors from North America, it took a while to accept the small, compact bedrooms and bathroom. Not an inch of space was wasted, with insufficient room to warrant the luxury of an armchair or desk. Despite being a four-star establishment, the floors were uneven; the toilet, when flushed, made considerable noise, as did the extractor fan; and although there were sufficient towels, space to hang these was at a premium. They telephoned the reception for more coat hangers, and decided to take a nap, setting alarms for five p.m.

Reluctantly waking when the alarm sounded, neither wanted to rise, with body clocks crying out that their beings needed more rest. While debating going back to sleep, Kate telephoned, cementing the decision to get up. They arranged to see her an hour later in the bar of her hotel, a short cab ride away. This rendezvous kicked them into action, and soon they found themselves sitting with Kate, delighted to be drinking cocktails with exotic names, courtesy of Kate's corporate credit card.

Although calling Vancouver home, the three only saw each other a few times a year. For some unexplained reason, it felt wrong when Jo was absent. There was a different dynamic. The group was incomplete and did not gel as well. The conversation flowed but not with the same rapport. They were a foursome, not a threesome, and this would always be the case. Daphne and Andrea complained about suffering jetlag and with the knowledge they would be meeting the next night, it was agreed the evening would not stretch on to the early hours. With intentions confirmed, they sat at the bar, finished the cocktails then ordered a bottle of wine and pizza.

Jo had already let it be known that her time was tight, but stressed they make no arrangements for the Thursday night before the opening ceremonies; the evening of the boat cruise. There were also plans for the four of them to get together the following night at a little Italian restaurant on the Earls Court Road, near where Daphne and Andrea were staying.

It had been arranged, following the river cruise, that they were to spend two nights in London, savouring the Olympic atmosphere, before heading to Amsterdam for a few nights. Daphne and Andrea were then returning directly to Vancouver, while Kate and Jo would remain in London to complete their work commitments to the Olympics. Kate was not planning to return until the Games were over. 'That is a very long time to be away', said Daphne, with more than a hint of jealousy. Kate acknowledged it was, but for the most part she did want to stay. While with Bob for over twenty years, thinking of him every day, and continuing to miss him, she was enjoying the single, independent life and adoring her work. The others teased her over whether this 'love of work' was related to a new love interest, but she said not and they believed her. It would be difficult to imagine a replacement for Bob in Kate's life.

Somewhat out of the blue, Daphne resurrected the conversation the four of them had about the menopause. She asked if they, too, felt that Jo had been a little too passionate and preoccupied — almost obsessive — with her discussion of the subject and the issues, when really it was not such a big deal. Kate immediately donned what the others referred to her 'counselling cap'. It was her understanding that women have radically different experiences to this changing hormonal balance. She recently read that Japanese women barely have any symptoms, but the same report confirmed that, at any one time, there were fifty million women in the world at menopausal age, and many of the symptoms experienced are severe. These statistics confirmed that there were bound to be huge differences. No two women were alike. Jo's experience seemed to imply she was on the extreme end of the scale, and if she was having problems, she needed the support of her friends; not their qualms or questions. She could get those from men.

Following her passionate retort, Kate wondered if she had over-stepped the mark with these words, which sounded like a lecture, but Daphne was keen to continue the conversation with Jo as the subject. 'She never really talks about David, does she?' said Daphne.

'But you don't talk about Kevin and I don't talk about Peter,' quipped Andrea, a little uncomfortable talking about her friend in her absence. Daphne backed off. Kate suggested the topic of husbands could be reserved for the following evening and joked that, to everyone's relief, she would therefore be silent.

It was getting late, but the hotel bar was still busy with international guests who, like Daphne and Andrea, were obviously on a different time zone. Crusts of pizza remained on the plate, so with the knowledge they would be drowning in the others' company over the forthcoming days, they said goodbye. The three women walked to the front of the hotel, arm in arm. Kate said goodbye and watched as her friends flagged a taxi, giggled, waved, and climbed into the back of the black car. Kate returned to the bar, signed for the food and wine, and headed for the elevator. She was not thinking of the women she had just spent the evening with, but of Jo and her nagging thoughts about the state of Jo's mind the last time they met. She believed Jo was an emotional time-bomb waiting to explode. She had been in control of her emotions in the past, but Kate was unsure whether this was the case now. Kate was aware that Jo was taking HRT and that it worked well in stabilising her moods, but what would she be like if this medication was denied, or if its effects wore off, or — as Jo had hinted — she simply decided, after two years on the medication, it was time to stop taking it. Kate knew her best friend very well. Unbeknown to Kate, this sequence of events was already in play.

Jo finished work at two p.m. and headed for her appointment with her doctor, Carol. She had been taking HRT for two years and knew the medication had been successful, but felt it was time to stop. As fate would have it, the day before the appointment she finished the tube of hormonal gel she applied daily to her skin, so it seemed like an ideal time. Arriving at Carol's office a few minutes late, she was told her appointment was cancelled as Carol's mother had been taken ill, requiring Carol to go to the hospital to deal with this crisis. Jo explained to the clearly stressed receptionist that she was busy with work and would call when things quietened down, to reschedule the appointment. It was not an urgent matter — more body maintenance than body cure. The receptionist, clearly delighted with this decision, quickly moved on to the next patient. Jo left, happy to have gained more time with her friends.

Although it was the height of the tourist season, with the Olympics only days away, the little Italian restaurant in which the women had arranged to meet that Monday evening was not busy. Jo had been an intermittent customer for years, originally introduced to it by a client, ten years ago. For as long as anyone could remember, the Napoli existed. Operated by an Italian couple in their eighties, and their son, who was probably sixty, the only other employees were two waitresses who were not young, coloured their hair jet black, yelled Italian loudly to each other and spoke heavily accented English to the diners. It was unclear if they were related to the family members. The staff never changed. The service was slow but attentive, and while the wait for the food could be considerable, the wine and breadsticks came quickly. Opera music played subtly in the background. Faded, dated images of Italian vineyards in the sunshine hid the rose wallpaper, which, to Jo's knowledge, had never been replaced. Nothing had changed in years. But the carpet was clean, the linen starched and the cutlery polished. This was not the place to dine if you had a theatre date, but ideal for four women wanting a quiet, reasonable, unpretentious place to eat, drink and enjoy each other's company without being asked to move on.

Two bottles of Chianti were ordered, along with appetisers; the wine promptly delivered as animated conversation commenced. Kate related anecdotes, but not names, of her colleagues and new international Olympic contacts; Daphne and Andrea spoke of jetlag, shopping, and how confusing they found the Underground, while Jo filled in the logistics of the boat cruise later that week. They were all to arrive at the quay by seven thirty p.m., for cocktails, and would sail at eight p.m. The tides were cooperating, enabling them to travel down the river to the Thames Barrier. There would be music, dancing and very few speeches but regrettably, no good-looking or available men.

The appetisers were presented on a huge decorative platter; prosciutto, ham, salamis, a variety of cheeses, olives, cherry tomatoes, roasted vegetables, shrimp, smoked salmon, artichokes and bread graced the plate. Another bottle of wine was ordered, as were glasses of water; tap water for everyone except Daphne, who requested sparkling. Kate steered the conversation to the subject of spouses. They quipped that as one of them did not have one of these 'useful' items, it was not a fair topic, but Jo's face changed. She obviously wanted this conversation.

'I'll start,' said Jo, looking at a piece of salami and not her friends. 'You know what I am about to say. You have all known for years and have been giving me advice. I just did not accept it. I do not love David at all.'

'So why don't you leave?' whispered Andrea. Jo looked up, reached for her wine, saying it just seemed easier to stay. She went on to explain that they rarely saw each other and lived — to all intents and purposes — separate lives, but if they did divorce, he would be the winner as her salary and bonuses were far greater than his. She would lose the house that she loved, and her pension. Jo looked away into the distance and — addressing the space, not her friends — told them of the other more important issue. She explained that in growing older, not a single day went by when she did not think how different her life would have been if David had been honest, and she had conceived. Heading towards retirement, she was finding her mind becoming preoccupied, almost obsessed, with the imminent loneliness of a life without children. Kate immediately wanted to challenge this view, and was about to give a lecture on the numerous women she knew — herself among them — who did not share this opinion, and whose lives were complete without offspring, when she saw the look of pain on Jo's face. This was a real, raw emotion her friend was experiencing. Better to remain silent.

Within what seemed like only seconds, Jo went from a calm, collected, intelligent businesswomen, rationally explaining the logistics of a boat cruise to her closest friends, to an emotional mess. With no forewarning, she started to sob, totally distraught, and searched for her purse under the table.

'Sorry, I thought I could talk about it. I wanted to be able to talk to you all, to share. I know I ought to — you are my best friends — but I cannot. It is so painful. I am not strong enough. I must go. I have to go: please let me. I'm sorry I ruined the night. I'll call tomorrow.'

They all stood up, speaking at once, offering comfort and support, and at the same time wondering how the evening could have so quickly spiralled downwards into this. They wanted her to stay and talk it out, knowing this would help, but Jo was adamant. This had never happened before and was out of character. Jo reached into her bag, retrieved three twenty-pound notes and flung them on the table. 'Please let me go. I need time alone... I'll be all right.' And with that, she walked quickly out of the restaurant.

It was only at this point that the three became aware the restaurant was completely quiet, as the patrons tried unsuccessfully to focus on their pastas and pizzas, fascinated by what was taking place between the well-dressed women seated at the table under the Venus statue. 'Well, I did not see that coming,' whispered Daphne, conscious of the audience.

'What just happened?' added Andrea, who looked close to tears, herself. Kate sighed and started to reveal the thoughts troubling her since the last time they all met in Vancouver, over a year ago.

Jo had stayed with her during the traumatic last days of Bob's life which, no matter how hard she tried, remained etched in fine detail in her memory. Living with someone, even if it was only for a few days, reaps a far deeper understanding of that being, whom you may have thought you had known well for years. Friends, Kate went on, are like onions — full of layers. You think you have peeled away all layers and know everything about them, but this is often an illusion. Even best friends have secrets. Kate explained that she saw Jo not only as a highly well-organised, accomplished, driven, intelligent women who was very capable, always willing to offer support to others, but also as a greatly stressed and emotional one. Jo's account of her hormonal journey added to Kate's understanding of her friend. The hormonal imbalance the menopause can create in some women was obviously affecting Jo badly. Now it would seem that Jo was beginning to obsess about her childlessness; an issue she had failed to address years ago when she should have. The loveless marriage added to her plight. Kate concluded to her friends that she held serious concerns regarding Jo's current mental state, especially if she had decided to stop taking her HRT medication, but did not know what to do.

Anyone would have difficulty having a rational, intelligent conversation after almost four bottles of Chianti, and for three emotional, tired women, this task was extreme. After Jo left, there was little appetite for the small amount of food remaining on their plates. They decided against entrée and dessert, but the proprietor arrived with a complementary serving of tiramisu and three forks. He had seen the outburst, did not try to understand it, but was sympathetic. It was not the first time a scene had occurred in his establishment and it would certainly not be the last. Kate asked for the bill. With little enthusiasm, they ate the desert, divided up the money Jo provided, and each put down a credit card to split payment. This necessitated complicated mathematical calculations for the old proprietor, and extended their departure by a further twenty minutes, which no one seemed to mind, least of all the other patrons who were looking for an encore. The old man eventually sought the support of the younger wine waiter, who could perform the necessary mathematical tasks and operate the Visa machine, so they were free to leave.

The friends stepped out of the air-conditioned restaurant, entering the noisy, sticky, busy street. The conversation developed to plans for the following day, whereupon Kate pulled a gilt-edged invitation from her purse for an afternoon champagne reception given by the Sochi Russia Olympic Organising Committee. 'This is my hard day tomorrow,' she teased.

Daphne snatched the invitation and read, 'Chief Inspector Katherine De Roche and Guest' and added 'Oh, can we come?'

Kate studied it. "I don't see why not,' she said, thinking they would both add some light relief and colour to what could be a very boring event. There then started a detailed discussion over what to wear for the Russians. Daphne exclaimed she had the most perfect red dress, to which Andrea quipped this was not at all a surprise. Daphne skipped down the street, invite in hand, as the others followed in her wake, creating a welcome, light distraction to the earlier intense emotions. Upon arriving at their hotel, Kate kissed her friends goodbye and took a cab back to her accommodation. Although tired, she decided to sit at the bar, ordered a liqueur coffee, not quite ready to retire.

There was a need to reflect on the evening. She would call Jo tomorrow, knowing it was better to not disturb her that night.

After leaving the Italian restaurant, Jo walked to the underground and took the Piccadilly line to the suburbs. She was hot and her heart was pounding. She searched for her reading glasses in the vain attempt to hide the fact she was crying. This futile effort at disguise did not matter: her fellow travellers, for the most part, were wrapped up in their own lives, not interested in that of a fifty-three-year-old, clearly distressed women. Alone in her own space, she tried to make sense of the outburst. It was out of character but a welcome release. She was among her best friends and would not be judged. They had all seen each other cry on numerous occasions; they had all revealed their deepest secrets to one another. There was nothing to be embarrassed or to apologise about.

As Jo walked towards her house, she saw the lights were on. David was home. When was the last time she had seen him? It was difficult to remember: maybe three or four days ago. Opening the door, she resented returning to a shared space, wanting to be alone, to sleep and wake to a new day, with the evening's outburst forgotten. She found him in the lounge, stretched out on the sofa; a pile of work papers showing graphs and figures on the coffee table, an empty beer can on the floor, and his laptop open. Despite the late hour, he appeared to be working.

'Hi,' she said. 'All good?'

'Fine,' he responded, not looking up. There was a silence and she waited for him to ask her where she had been, or how she had been, or whether she had remembered to buy milk or the light bulb the wardrobe needed, but he said nothing. Eventually, he put his pen down and looked at her, asking if there was any possibility, she could get a few more tickets for the river cruise, as he would like to invite a couple of colleagues to make the evening bearable, he added. Jo sighed and said she thought he understood this was her company's flagship event and there were no spare tickets. It was even risky for her to invite personal friends. Looking annoyed, he returned to his papers.

'I'm going to bed. I have a full day tomorrow,' Jo said. David added that he had things to do but would be home for the rest of the week. This was not welcome news.

Kate wanted to telephone Jo, late in the morning, the following day but despite the best intentions, a busy schedule denied the opportunity. Her morning saw a rather boring tour of the new Olympic Stadium, given by a man wearing a crumpled, dated suit who dryly informed the group of an array of unconnected facts about the building. He was preoccupied by the amount of concrete used, the unusual metal fortification applied in the construction, the washroom and catering capacity, as well as the security system and evacuation procedures. Thankfully, the tour was over within two hours. The afternoon consisted of the reception given by the Soviet delegation.

The Russian event could not be missed, having been spoken about amongst her colleagues since being announced weeks ago, when they were still in Canada. Everyone knew the next Olympic Games in Sochi, Russia, would be the most lavish ever. Russian President Vladimir Putin decreed it would occur in the resort town of Sochi, which many believed did not have the climate for a Winter Olympics, being described by some as a subtropical seaside resort. This scepticism was banished when a budget of over US$ 50 billion was announced. The afternoon reception was being held in the penthouse suite of a designer hotel on the edge of the Thames; a hotel built and operated by a Russian businessman, who not only owned this hotel, but whose company was building over fifty per cent of the new hotels currently under construction in Sochi. No expense was to be spared for this function.

Kate found her friends in the sumptuous lobby of the hotel, lost in the padded sofa, admiring the huge vases of fresh flowers. The aroma was intoxicating. There were mirrors and sculptures everywhere, creating the illusion that the space was far larger than it was. The concierge glanced at Kate's invitation and directed the women to the elevator, which would deliver them to the top floor. Upon entering, they found a uniformed man whose only function was to ensure they arrived at the destination. In a matter of seconds, the doors opened and they stepped directly into the reception. Andrea let out an audible gasp and grasped Kate's arm. The room consisted of floor-to-ceiling windows on three walls. On one side, transparent shades had been lowered as the sun was bright, but this did not detract from the views from a sixty-fifth-floor elevation. The London skyline looked spectacular.

A deep Persian carpet covered the floor, contemporary art decorated the wall and high circular tables had been strategically placed for guests to congregate at, each covered with promotional leaflets for the Sochi Olympics. There were huge ice sculptures in the shape of eagles and swans, and every type of alcohol imaginable on offer at the bar, including at least twenty varieties of vodka. Suited waiters circulated with silver trays of champagne flutes. Caviar, canapés and an array of finger food were offered on large platters by skinny women wearing high-heeled shoes and a lot of make-up. This party, claimed as the most lavish to take place during the next two weeks, was certainly living up to the boast.

Most of the approximately one hundred attendees were suited men. The entrance, from the elevator, of three well-dressed, attractive women caused a small hesitation in conversations as the new arrivals were examined.

'Recognise anyone?' Andrea whispered to Kate, who shook her head. A tray of champagne glasses was immediately presented and taking a glass each, they moved into the room, settling at one of the high circular tables offering the literature. The women started to study the party. They recognised one easily identifiable group as the British contingency, congregating in a corner, all looking a little sheepish and uncomfortable. This was supposed to be weeks of celebrations showcasing their country. This afternoon, they had been completely usurped.

A tall, well-dressed man made his way over with an air of confidence only the host of such an event could display. He had a full head of grey, curly hair, wore a well-cut suit, a tie with gold tie-pin and shiny leather shoes with pointed toes, making his feet seem awfully long. His face was a little pock-marked from juvenile acne, but the blue eyes soon distracted the observer from the blemishes. He introduced himself as Igor Rakanowski, part of the organising committee for the forthcoming Sochi Olympics, and one of the hosts for the afternoon. Kate took the lead, thanking him for the invite and explaining who she was, then introduced Andrea and Daphne. Although polite in his greetings, nothing could disguise the fact that his attention was centred on Daphne. Kate and Andrea glanced at each other as Igor directed his conversation towards their friend. Wearing a striking, deep red, silk, wraparound dress, with a deep V-neck, (which necessitated the use of sticky tape and some strategically placed safety pins applied by Andrea earlier in the day, to ensure it did not fall open), high-heeled gold shoes and with her long blonde hair tied back with gold clips, Daphne clearly outshone Kate, in her smart, grey trouser suit, and Andrea, in yellow, silk blouse and black pants. They did not mind. This was not the first time this had occurred, and it would certainly not be the last. Daphne started to discuss the wonderful vista the venue awarded, and soon found herself being led by the arm to the window for a clearer view. She returned to her friends a few minutes later, with the news that Igor was not only part of the Sochi Committee but was a partner in the building of a number of the hotels in construction for the Sochi Games, and had a role in building this one, playfully adding he also seemed 'really nice.'

Kate recognised a few faces from the International Police Federation in the room, excused herself from her friends and went over to reconnect. The reception seemed a little strained at first, but as the afternoon progressed and the champagne flowed, so did the conversation. Everyone spoke English and although many attendees used their first language among colleagues, they were at ease switching to English when joined by others from different countries. Kate spoke only English, and continued to be impressed by those who could easily switch tongues with what seemed like no effort. She turned back to look for her friends, observing that Igor had, again, come over to talk to

Daphne and Andrea. Andrea shot her a glance which said, 'Save me' and walked away from the couple, who did not notice her move.

'So, he does genuinely seem like a nice guy,' Andrea revealed to Kate, replacing an empty glass on the passing tray, taking another and grinning at the waiter, who smiled back. She realised that the alcohol and the consumption of only light food were having an effect, but quite liked the whole scene, and was not thinking of any consequences. The women sat on stools at one of the high tables, casually watching their friend and the flirty gestures of a couple who were obviously enjoying each other's company. They both knew Daphne could use some fun in her life from a genuinely nice man.

The afternoon was drawing on with no attempt by the hosts to terminate the affair. The waitresses continued to circulate, although the demand for food was now non-existent; the sound of the uncorking of champagne bottles audible above the increasing noise in the room. It seemed everyone was having a good time with no desire to retire. Only the British group had left. The hosts were satisfied; Igor specifically so. It was only when telling Andrea she needed to find the washroom and realising that she was swaying, walking across the carpet, that Kate looked at her watch. It was six p.m. They had been drinking champagne for four hours. It was time to go home.

Returning to the reception, she found Andrea, Daphne and Igor engaged in conversation about the opening ceremonies. Igor would be attending and had spare tickets, but the women declined his offer. As they all walked towards the elevator, Igor took Daphne aside. She returned a few moments later and they entered the elevator.

'We are having afternoon tea here tomorrow, and he is going to show me around,' she beamed. Her friends both smiled. Daphne retorted it was not like anything they were thinking, and he was just being nice, but the perpetual grin and glow easily gave her away.

The fresh air hit them as they left the hotel, and with the realisation they had been drinking for hours, the objective was solely to return to their hotels as quickly as possible and sleep. Any thoughts of contacting Jo were forgotten in a drunken champagne haze.

Kate woke at three a.m., throat dry, and for the briefest of moments was oblivious to the events of the preceding afternoon. Wanting to go back to sleep but knowing this to be naïve, as her bladder and head were throbbing, she got up and headed towards the bathroom, half cognisant of the clothes strewn across the floor. She wondered if she had remembered to return with her purse, or if it remained in the back of a taxi somewhere in London. After visiting the bathroom, emptying her bladder, searching for the required medication and attempting to drink a full glass of water, she returned to bed, trying to remember what was required of her the following day. She could not. Switching on the light, she set the alarm for seven a.m. and attempted to sleep, telling herself, not for the first time, she was too old to consume large amounts of alcohol.

Jo was sitting in her office when the phone rang. It had been two days since the meltdown in the Italian restaurant and, in that time, she had not replied to the numerous phone messages her friends left. At her desk, at this moment, she was not thinking of her girlfriends or work, but of a child she had never met, diagnosed with leukaemia. The child was the daughter of the women who cleaned her office; a person she did not know well as their paths rarely crossed. She heard the tragic news from Audrey, who occupied the front desk and was Holden Sealants' one-woman news anchor. There was not much happening in the organisation that Audrey did not know about. It was rumoured, in the early days of the company, that Audrey had been romantically involved with Bernard; something she hinted at, but never confirmed. Jo always passed the time of day with Audrey, recognising that in an organisation such as Holden, being in Audrey's good books was just as important as reaching sales targets and not crashing into the CEO's BMW when parking in the office carpark. Jo expressed concern to Audrey, telling her to convey her sympathies to the cleaner, whose name she had already forgotten, and quickly headed towards her office, tears welling in her eyes. Upon entering, she hastily closed the door and sat down. She knew this was a complete over-reaction, but one she was unable to control. At this moment the telephone rang, and Kate's voice was heard. Jo made a vain attempt at composure, which Kate saw through but decided not to question. Apologising for the evenings events, Jo told her friend she was fine, just a bit tired and stressed with all the arrangements for the cruise. She cut the conversation short with the excuse of an imminent meeting and ended the call. Kate understood her friend well, knowing when not to push. After reconfirming the arrangements for the boat trip, she said goodbye. Gossip about Daphne and Igor could wait.

Jo left her office just before four p.m., telling colleagues and Audrey to contact her if there were any issues with arrangements for the following day, no matter how small. Audrey assured her everything would be fine and in her maternal way, directed her to get an early night as she would need all her energy tomorrow. Jo thanked her, then drove home in a haze, going over every detail of the forthcoming event, ensuring every base was covered. Stopping at a traffic light, she watched a young couple cross the road, each holding the hand of a small, red-headed, impish-looking boy. The child was about six years old, wearing a red Manchester United football shirt and black shorts, demanding his parents lift him high into the air and swing him as they walked along. They obliged, prompting him to laugh and plead the action be repeated. Jo watched as the happy family passed in front of her car. The lights turned green but were blurry. She was again in tears. There was a loud blast on a horn and Jo realised she was not moving, so drove on, avoiding the temptation to take another look at the happy child. She arrived home thirty minutes later, sobbing to such an extent that her chest hurt.

David's car was in the driveway. Taking a deep breath, she got out of her vehicle and walked up the path to the front door. His case was in the hallway. Entering the kitchen, she put her purse on the counter, which was covered with toast crumbs. David had a habit of eating toast without a plate, while reading emails on his phone over the counter. She could see the image in her mind's eye, knowing his traits so well.

Yelling his name, there was no response. The house was empty: a blessing. She could cry in peace. It was only five p.m. — early for a drink — but she opened the fridge, found an opened bottle of wine and poured a large glass, drinking it as if it was water. She started to tidy the kitchen, putting away the bread and jam, wiping counter tops, emptying the dishwasher. During all these tasks the tears did not subside. These jobs completed, she went upstairs, closed the bedroom curtains in a hopeless attempt to darken the room, took off her clothes and got into bed, crying herself to sleep.

She woke, at eight thirty p.m., upon hearing the front door slam. Getting up, she looked at her red eyes; any traces of make-up washed away. Pulling on her dressing gown, she headed downstairs. David was in the kitchen, flicking through a magazine. 'Where have you been?' she asked.

'Next door,' he responded, not looking up but moving towards the toaster where he had already placed two slices of bread. He continued, 'Gillian had a drain back-up so I took some of that drain de-blocker round for her, and Ken arrived home, so we ended up having a few beers, but no food.'

He removed the slices of toast and immediately took a bite of one. Looking at her for the first time and with a full mouth, he said, 'My God, you look rough.' Jo's shoulders started shaking, the tears falling as she explained about the little red-haired boy looking so happy with his parents, and how it had opened the wounds she had about children. David's lie had initially been devastating, but she had learned to live with it; his affairs she believed were short-lived one-night stands and had been tolerable, but more recently her resentment had been increasing. For some reason, the events she lived with for years were gaining a new significance. They could no longer remain unchallenged. Growing older and reflecting on her life and its direction had become a preoccupation. These tears were his fault. Her heartache was his fault. The emptiness and loneliness she had, and would have for the rest of her life, were his fault. God damnit, even crumbs on the kitchen floor were his fault. She wanted him to admit he lied. If he could do this, they could perhaps move on. David turned away.

'Not that again,' he said, walking out of the kitchen, leaving her alone.

The entrance to the Grand Hotel was large and imposing. Two men in long heavy coats, totally inappropriate for the time of year, were positioned to open the doors leading to the lobby. It was four p.m. Daphne was never late. Igor was seated, looking at the entrance, when she entered. He walked confidently towards her. Heads turned. Daphne had chosen her outfit carefully, as anyone would if they were about to embark on their first date in twenty years. Wide-legged, navy-blue linen pants with a cream silk blouse, under which a lacey camisole could teasingly be seen. Her nipples could not. Salmon-coloured Coach pump shoes provided the contrast to the high-heeled, gold footwear she wore when they met. The outfit was not as elaborate as the previous day's red dress; it was more serious, but still sophisticated and sexy. It was also chosen as it could easily be removed; no tape or squeezing, uncomfortable underwear required. A simple gold chain was the only jewellery. She had not removed her wedding ring and if asked, planned to tell Igor of her marriage and children. They danced around the subject the previous day, but she did not want there to be secrets.

Igor obviously knew his way around and everyone seemed to acknowledge him. The maître d' showed them to a small, quiet alcove away from the tables of Japanese tourists. A waitress arrived and Igor ordered. There was no problem thinking of subjects to discuss, and he seemed to really enjoy talking to her, always holding her in his gaze, never looking bored or becoming distracted, genuinely interested in every aspect of her life; verbal flirting of the sort she had never encountered before.

The last thing Daphne wanted was for the afternoon to finish, but after two hours the salon was almost empty and she was conscious that the waiting staff were circulating. Reading her mind — he seemed quite good at this — Igor asked if she had any plans for the evening. She did not. If being perfectly honest, she wanted to have sex with him but she did not have the confidence to articulate this desire, nor knew how to. He looked a little sheepish and said he was sure they could prolong their time together in a suite in the hotel, and maybe have some champagne and strawberries delivered. How was she to respond to this request with a cool detachment when this man had read her thoughts? There were no rules. She smiled, agreeing that would be lovely. He stood up and led her to the reception, where he quickly gained a couple of key cards to one of the suites on the top floor; not the best, he apologised to her, those were occupied by some prince from India, here for the Olympics, but he was sure she would approve.

The champagne was already on ice in the lounge area when they entered. The blue and green, silk, floral wallpaper with peacocks and other exotic birds mirrored the colour of the drapes and carpet. This lavish, opulent, interior design was not one Daphne specifically liked, but could easily tolerate. She excused herself to use the washroom, which was as large as any hotel bedroom she had stayed in. Sitting on the toilet, she stared and smiled at her reflection in the floor-to-ceiling mirror-tiled wall. Dressed, sober, about to enter a bedroom for maybe one hour (how she hoped not) or ten, she sat, wanting to prolong the inevitable, to drown in the moment. Studying her reflection, she grinned at the knowledge of what was bound to come next, wanting this brief 'before' time to last forever. The anticipation, the excitement, the sex with a body not familiar to her, the exploration, the not knowing what he would do next, nor what she would do next. Surely this was about to become the best day of her life.

She returned as Igor was pouring two flutes of champagne. He had removed his jacket and shoes and handing her a glass, led her into the bedroom. He placed his glass on the bedside table, lay on his back on the bed and suggested she did the same. She did, kicking off her shoes as she did so. They lay next to each other. No contact; the sexual energy palpable. They could hear some noise in the corridor outside, which soon abated. They lay in silence. She felt his fingers touch hers and soon they were entwined. He started to play with her wedding ring, twisting it around.

'You are a married lady,' he eventually ventured. It was not a question. It was a statement.

'I am a very unhappily married lady,' she responded. More silence. Her heart pounded as she felt herself becoming hotter, blood racing around her body. She considered leaping on top of him and taking the lead at this seduction, which he was obviously nervous about. Her desire was building. Forthright sex looked far more appealing than the conversations they were about to embark on.

'I am sure it is very complicated, and I only want to know what you want to tell me,' he said. His fingers had left her ring and were now subtly stroking her forearm. She internally screamed for them to move to her breasts and rolled onto her side to encourage the action, but he was reluctant to pick up the telepathy, no matter how she altered her position.

'I think we could be very good friends,' he said, as her heart exploded, face blushed and vaginal juices soaked her underwear. Had anyone ever been led on so far before intercourse? Had anyone ever felt such an intense sexual surge with so little physical contact? Why did he still want to talk? The anticipation was unbearable.

She took the lead, moved onto her side to be closer to him and leaned towards his face, gently stroking his lips with hers. Not a kiss, more of a brush, pressing the breasts, still yearning for attention, into his chest. He responded, gently pulling her on top of him. After a short time, the brushing progressed to passionate kissing, then suddenly he stopped, put his hands on her shoulders and pushed her back. Oh my God, she thought: he wants to start a conversation again. How could this be prevented? With a serious look on his face, he said, almost sheepishly, 'I have not done this for a very long time.'

She smiled. 'Well, I have not *wanted* to do this for a very long time.' They laughed.

'Would you like to get undressed?' he politely asked. Her nipples hardened and she got up, took a gulp of champagne and started to hastily unbutton her blouse. He did the same. At last, the best day of her life was about to happen.

Jo arrived at Westminster Pier at seven p.m., immediately spotting Michael in animated conversation with a man in a starched white shirt with epaulettes: the captain, she presumed. Michael was wearing a tuxedo with a yellow bow tie, corresponding exactly to the corporate colour used for the Holden Sealants logo. Going that extra mile for the client, she smiled. Although it was an hour before they were due to sail, Jo had requested her organising committee arrive early to address any last-minute issues and be ready to greet the guests. The weather was accommodating — a warm summer evening, not too hot, with a slight breeze.

Michael was eager to give his five clients a brief tour, and introduced them to the captain, crew, waiting staff, bar staff and chef. Everything seemed in hand and Jo relaxed, feeling this was money well-spent. She took a glass of Prosecco and sat down on one of the red velvet sofas that ringed the edge of the room, studying the space for any obvious flaws.

Michael suddenly reappeared at her side.

'There is always something,' he exclaimed. Jo's calm composure melted as she sat, dreading his next statement. Seeing her reaction, Michael put his arm around her shoulder, squeezing it gently.

'Oh, no — nothing that dramatic,' he added. He went on to explain that the CCTV cameras were covered with seagull shit, so they were next to useless, and the company supposed to clean them earlier in the day had not arrived, having a more pressing Olympic Games client. He explained that it was supposedly illegal to sail without operational cameras, but the Thames seagulls love his boat with the high camera perches, presenting a perpetual issue.

'You would just not believe how much they shit!' he concluded, saying it was nothing to concern her and would not affect the evening, as he got up and headed towards the kitchens, blowing her a kiss as he went.

The boat's external masts and deck were adorned with lights. Inside, there was a large seating area, a small dance floor, and a podium displaying the Holden Sealants logo, from where there would be speeches.

Holden Sealants banners, promoting various brands of sealant — all-weather, coloured, ultra-white — were on display, ensuring no one was unaware who was sponsoring the event. A raffle had been arranged with guests encouraged to deposit business cards into a glass jar upon entering. Later in the evening, a winner would be chosen. The first prize was an all-expenses trip for two to Las Vegas and the 2013 National Hardware Show — a three-day annual trade event held in May every year. Two tickets for the Olympic opening ceremonies were also on offer. The draw was to take place towards the end of the evening when the vessel was on its return journey, the sun had gone down and the few sanctioned speeches completed. Michael agreed to act as compere, a role he had obviously performed before, was keen to do, and which Jo imagined he would be particularly good at. She was to have no part in the presentation.

The guests started to arrive at seven fifteen p.m. David, Kate, Daphne, and Andrea arrived together, having met in a pub an hour earlier. They all appreciated that this was Jo's night and she should be left alone. She greeted them immediately, realising David was a little drunk, confirmed by Andrea's body language towards him. They stepped on board and each took a glass of wine. She regretted including him, as he half-heartedly placed a kiss on her cheek then moved away, slightly unstable. Tears started to well in her eyes at this gesture. There really was no love left. She had not cried all day, so why now?

'Get a grip girl,' she told herself, knowing — deep down — this would be difficult. If someone said the wrong thing to her, she could fall apart. Maybe it was not the right time to quit HRT, she fleetingly thought.

More guests were arriving now, as it was seven thirty. Michael Bublé, Adele, and Ed Sheerin mixed with Elton John, Dire Straits, and the Police; a selection of music from different eras, to accommodate the mixture of age groups, played in the background. Many took their drinks outside, although space was limited. Others secured tables inside, with friends and colleagues, and seemed set for the night. Bernard's loud laugh could be heard bellowing from the bar. With a large blast of the horn, the boat pulled away from the dock and Captain Morris welcomed everyone aboard. There followed the obligatory announcement concerning the location of life jackets and evacuation procedures, talked over and ignored. The crowd at the bar subsided, the kitchen doors rapidly swung forwards and backwards, as trays of food were delivered and replenished. Michael had explained that it was preferable to feed everyone immediately to soak up the alcohol and prevent any sea sickness. The vessel passed the London Eye.

Jo spent her time greeting guests, introducing people and trying not to forget names. A few years ago, she never forgot a name — now it seemed to happen frequently, even with people known for a long-time. Memory lapses occurred on a regular basis, she noticed.

Periodically, Captain Morris would announce the cruise was passing another monument — Canary Wharf, St. Paul's Cathedral, the Tower of London. The guests showed no interest in these sights: they were here for the food, the alcohol and the party. They knew about London.

By the time the excursion reached its destination — the Thames Barrier — the sun had almost set. It had become cooler and there was a breeze, so most guests returned inside. Plates were being cleared away. There was still food on the buffet table but few takers, except for David, who was by himself and finding it difficult to hold a plate of food and a glass of alcohol at the same time, and remain vertical. Jo was annoyed and went over to him, taking his plate. She guided him towards the outside deck, pretending to show affection, but rage was building with every step taken, quietly instructing him to take deep breaths. Leaving him outside, she returned to view the crowd, spotting her girlfriends in the corner talking to Liam, the Northern Ireland sales representative, and his wife. Liam was a great character, having been with the company many years, and the reason sales of Holden Sealants in Northern Ireland were so strong. She hoped he would never be tempted to leave. He greeted her with a kiss on the cheek, then whispered to her, out of hearing of the others, that David seemed to be looking rough and did she want him to act. She stated, probably too strongly, that David was not his problem and he should remain where he was, have a good time and forget about her drunken husband. Liam backed off. Relieved, he turned his attention to the group.

Michael stepped towards the microphone and following a few attempts to silence the crowd, announced that in five minutes they would be starting the formal part of the evening, assuring everyone the presentations would not take long, after which they would be drawing for the raffle. The few people remaining outside were encouraged to enter the body of the party.

Jo excused herself from her friends to ensure that Bernard was ready to speak. He was deep in conversation and picking up on his body language, which basically said 'I know what I'm doing', she withdrew. The salon was getting hot and loud. She headed for the outside deck just as Michael was returning to the microphone. Pausing, she watched as he provoked the crowd with some polite back-and-forth banter. Once again, Jo congratulated herself on the way the evening was progressing and left for some fresh air.

The deck was subtly lit; the rhythmic sound of the engines soothing. It seemed the vessel was travelling quite quickly; certainly faster, than on the outward journey, but this could have been the effect of the night sky. The Thames was dark, almost black, and there were few other vessels in view. A burst of laughter, followed by applause, disturbed her tranquillity and she wiped water from her eye, not even realising she had started to cry — again. Looking towards the stern, she noticed someone leaning over the barrier, obviously vomiting into the water. She stood for a moment, assessing the scene. Other than her, he was the only one present. She, of course, knew who it was. It was the man who denied her children, lied to her, slept with other women, spent her money, ruined her life. It was a small, drunk man who could not swim. She silently approached him. As she got closer, she could see him swaying, hear him retching, smell his vomit. How amazingly easy, she thought, as she flung her arms around his thighs, adopting the rugby-tackle lunge she remembered from her youth, grabbed him and threw him over the boat's low barrier into the water below.

As David's body tumbled, without ceremony, into the water, there was a thud, a splash, then only the sound of the boat's engine. Jo was rational. He was drunk: he could not swim. They were in a wide section of the Thames with no other vessels close by. There were no operational CCTV cameras. If he did survive, no one would know it was her. If he did not, she would have won the gold medal. Had she not been thinking of this event for years? She was strangely terrified but elated at the same time; more applause from below, as her audience obviously agreed. Jo turned and headed back to the party. The draw for the Vegas trip was under way and Michael was joking that the winner need not attend the National Hardware Show as there were a few other things Las Vegas was famous for. Jo knew that no matter how tempting Vegas was, her colleagues were already salivating at the idea of the large collection of home improvement, building and gardening supplies in one space. The prize was awarded to a couple from Scotland, who owned several independent building supplies stores in remote communities. The winner tried to look happy, but his wife was clearly apprehensive: this trip to London could easily have been the furthest they had travelled. Vegas was far beyond their comfort zone. Neither seemed to want to spend beyond the briefest of moments accepting the award. Michael read the situation well, announcing there were only forty minutes until they docked, advising everyone to make the most of the bar and the dance floor as the volume increased and David Bowie yelled 'Let's Dance.' Jo went over to Kate. 'I need to talk to you now.' Kate immediately recognised something was seriously wrong and followed her friend outside.

They were not alone. Some others ventured onto the deck to smoke, kiss, cool down, escape the loud music, and appreciate the London skyline. The women headed to a bench seat away from anyone's hearing, as Jo explained to her best friend what she had done. Upon reflection, Kate could not believe just how calm they both were at this time.

'What do I do now?' Jo asked. Kate bit her lip, her mind racing. A senior police officer informed of a murder (or attempted murder) is seriously thinking how it can be covered up. The perpetrator, also her best friend, assisted her in the killing of her spouse less than two years ago. Could this be happening? Kate told herself to think rationally. Several people had witnessed David's drunken state. Liam advised him to take fresh air and go outside. The barrier he was leaning against was low; looking at the water below can easily become hypnotising. He fell overboard and drowned. It was an accident. And finally, as she knew only too well, it would receive minimal attention as everyone's thoughts were preoccupied with the Olympics, due to formally start in a few hours' time.

The vessel was slowing as they approached Westminster Quay. The crew had used a handheld device to count the passengers onto the boat. Would they use the same device to count people off, and if they did, how reliable was this method?

'We have to wait until everyone has got off and then inform Michael and the captain that we cannot find him, but also say he may have already got off. We cannot tell Daphne or Andrea — better that fewer people know.' Jo followed Kate's instructions and began to move away and resume her role as the organiser of a successful night. Bernard sought her out, obviously delighted, as his wife tried to lead him away, conscious of his garrulous, drunken self, and the late hour. Kate watched, marvelling at her friend's composure as she worked the room. Michael arrived, glass of wine in hand, his first sip of alcohol that evening, relaxing as the event was winding down. He embraced Jo and sought her confirmation that all had gone well. It was easy to oblige.

Jo casually asked if he had seen her spouse, as she had not seen him leave and could not locate him. The crew were busily clearing up, stacking chairs, collecting glasses, gathering discarded napkins, anxious for the evening to end and get home. There was a crash in the kitchen, followed by loud voices. Michael sighed, said he would be in touch, kissed her lightly on the cheek and headed towards the kitchen, gulping wine as he went. As an after-thought, he turned, confirming he had not seen David.

Jo returned to her friends. Daphne and Andrea offered a half-hearted assurance that David would turn up, but there was an odd tension in the group. They walked in silence up the gang plank and onto the quay, all knowing he would not easily be found. Daphne's face lit up at the sight of Igor leaning against a large, black car, illegally parked.

'Taxis are so difficult to get during the Olympics, so I thought you would appreciate a ride home.'

Jo quickly said she was fine on the tube, embraced her friends and moved away, eager to be alone, away from the vessel and the scene of the crime. She had, of course. heard of Igor and his influence on her friend, but this was not the time to get to know him. She walked the short distance along the banks of the Thames to the Underground station, while the others were assisted into the back of the chauffeur- driven car.

When Kate's phone rang at seven a.m. the following day, she immediately knew who was calling. It was the day of the opening ceremonies, and all the available police and security services, including the Port of London Authority with jurisdiction for the Thames, were on high alert. Kate understood a missing person, last seen drunk on a pleasure cruiser with one hundred and fifty others who had also been drinking, would warrant only the necessary paperwork and sympathetic looks towards a reporting family member. Jo's local police station, in the suburbs, would be quieter than one in Central London, so Kate advised going to the one nearest the boat's quay in Westminster. She told Jo to come to her hotel so they would both go together to file the report.

Jo had always been a rational, intelligent being. She had not slept all night and while awake, attempted to analyse how she could have committed such a radical action. It had not been planned. She had not boarded the vessel knowing she was about to murder her spouse. After hours of wakefulness, she was starting to correlate her extreme actions of the previous night with her changed emotional state. Having not taken any pills or applied the hormonal replacement gel for the last week, she recognised that her being had altered during this time. She was more unstable, irrational, impetuous, emotional, tearful and extremely hot. The actions of last night had been building for years. They could not be directly related to her decision to stop taking hormone replacements, but maybe this decision contributed to her fragile mental state and subsequent actions. She called Carol's direct line, knowing she would be in the office, and requested a prescription be faxed to her twenty-four-hour pharmacy. Jo picked up the drugs at eight thirty a.m., and sat in her car applying the hormonal gel to her forearms, immediately feeling the calming magic taking effect; the magic that would treat a generation of women lucky enough to access it.

David's body was found three days later, washed up on the muddy banks of the Thames, not far from Greenwich. The coroner quickly filed a report, stating it was his opinion that the death was accidental, with the victim falling from a pleasure cruiser having consumed a considerable amount of alcohol. He had hit his head when falling and was unconscious when entering the water, where he subsequently drowned. Jo received the news on the Sunday morning while watching a cookery programme on television and preparing for her brief trip to Amsterdam. Two police officers — one male, one female — arrived at her house and relayed the facts while standing in her kitchen. Jo had not invited them to sit down, nor offered tea or coffee. They asked if she needed someone from Victim Services to contact her. She confirmed she did not, adding she had three fantastic female friends, who would always be there for her. The officers left. She finished packing with a smile on her face, not having cried for two days.

Chapter 4
Hot, Cool, Yours
Sochi, Winter Olympics 2014

Igor sat in an executive box at Olympic Park, the brand-new stadium constructed for the Games in London, on the first Monday morning of the much-anticipated 2012 Summer Games. He was one of an elite few invited to watch the Track and Field events from this prestigious vantage point, but he lacked the enthusiasm displayed by his fellow citizens, who also received the much-coveted invitations. The box was decorated with images of polar bears, snow hares and snow leopards; the mascots of the forthcoming Sochi Olympics. The spectators were primarily loud, patriotic, male Russians. Having rejected the champagne and array of designer vodkas, and ignoring the buffet table, Igor settled himself away from the throng in a large, high- backed, leather armchair with a cup of herbal tea and a copy of Pravda, the Russian newspaper formerly associated with the Communist Party, that he continued to read out of habit. Today, the words and stories it held had little interest. Like the sporting events taking place in the stadium below, world events were occurring without scratching the surface of his consciousness. His total being was interested only in one thing, one being, one woman: Daphne.

He had last seen her the previous Thursday evening, when driving her back to her hotel following the boat cruise. Her friends tactfully left, and he remained alone with her in his car. They had spent a wonderful three days in each other's company. He could not remember a time in his life when he was as happy. Everything was perfect. At this point, he was sure the chemistry, commitment and deep love he felt was mutual, confidently believing she wanted to be included in his plans for them to start an existence together in Sochi, or Vancouver, and share their future lives. There was nothing he could not offer her, and she had already explained, in no uncertain terms, she had no love for her abusive, alcoholic husband. He had never felt this way about anyone before and was sure, following their intense time together, she shared his emotions. It was, therefore, a complete surprise when his proposal was rejected. She admitted there was a deep affection, and if they did not live ten thousand miles apart, and she was not married, and did not have three children whom she adored and who needed her, then things would have been different, but at this point there could be no future. Acknowledging the last few days had been fun, confessing they were some of the best, in her life, she remained resolute that the relationship was over. He asked her not to go to Amsterdam, and at least spend the following few days with him but she would not, implying that her girlfriends had priority over him; a sentiment he found impossible to understand. How can female friendship override love? In a cold, rational way, he found her intentions incomprehensible and totally devastating. With no more to say she left his car, and his life.

He cried as he watched her leave. The whole encounter could not be understood nor believed. Never had he been so much in love. At forty-nine years old, there had been a few girlfriends but he had not experienced this total infatuation for anyone before. And it was an infatuation; an obsession. A curse. He had spent the last four days thinking of nothing but Daphne. Totally out of character.

Staring blankly through the glass windows, he watched the athletes below, jealous of their minds and their bodies, geared to easily achievable goals. If they could train to be the fittest, or the strongest, or the fastest, they would win and be awarded the prize they sought. His prize was far more elusive. What were the rules of the game he needed to play to obtain her? These were not defined. He could not win a contest where the criteria were unspecified. He had been accomplished in business, having succeeded in that arena on every occasion. He was finding it impossible to accept losing in the arena of love.

The tea remained untouched. Loud conversations were taking place and periodically there were gasps, laughter and applause as the enthusiastic audience watched the proceedings below, but he remained totally detached from the surroundings. Why had he even come? She would be in Amsterdam now with her friends and, in a few days, return to Vancouver. There were no plans for them to ever meet again. This could not be happening. Tears started to prick his eyes, knowing he should be rational in his behaviour but having barely slept in the last week, these tears a manifestation of this fatigued state and persistent, deep self-pity. This was not a rational love. There was no 'getting over' this. He could not simply 'pull himself together' and move on easily. It would take a lifetime, or radical action.

'Igor!'

His introspective thoughts were suddenly broken by the loud, commanding voice of Rupert, a Russian property developer he had known for several years, and whom he quite liked, but rarely encountered. Rupert had attended the same high school as Igor, on the outskirts of Moscow, but was a couple of years older. While at school, Rupert had the reputation of being a little eccentric. It was rumoured he kept snakes, could speak five languages, and was the son of a Russian count — who lived abroad — and a Portuguese gymnast, but no one could add any firm facts to these claims, and Rupert offered no clues. Igor also heard that Rupert had his heart broken in his early twenties and never recovered, and this was the reason he remained a confirmed bachelor, having spent several years abroad. He apparently named one of his hotels after this first love — Rosa. Rupert approached, precariously balancing a large plate of marinated fish and a glass of champagne, obviously delighted to have found someone in the gathering he knew. Without invitation, he pulled a chair closer to Igor, obliviously spilling fish on the carpet as he did so. Then, with a huge grin on his face, he started to engage in animated conversation. 'Wonderful venue, don't you think? But, of course, ours will be way better,' he boasted.

Igor gave a half-hearted smile, wondering if he should encourage this interaction in an attempt to escape the melancholy state endured for days, or be rude so that he could continue to bask in the selfish sadness that was becoming the new normal. Rupert quickly read the situation and, in a refreshing though tactless way, still chewing his fish, he asked why Igor was not in the thick of the crowd, enjoying the spectacle and the champagne. Igor could have brushed off the comment, or made an excuse to leave, but recognised that he needed to talk. Maybe Rupert would be able to offer the third-person reasoning he desperately needed. At the very least, he would be a distraction. After four days of being alone, with only the thoughts of Daphne, it was time to share. And so, while the other guests in the elite box took full advantage of the champagne and cocktails, ate pâté and caviar, and watched the best athletes in the world compete for their countries to obtain the much-coveted medals, Igor poured out his love obsession to Rupert.

Both men benefitted from the frank, unusual interaction: Igor, because he could rationally explain his emotions to a contemporary; and Rupert, because he felt useful in being able to offer advice to someone he liked, with whom he shared a common background, and who clearly needed and was ready to accept his opinions. He could act as the father, the teacher, the older statesman with unspecified qualifications, to offer sage counsel. The role felt good.

Rupert was an optimist, like Igor, seeing his personal wealth grow significantly since the fall of the Soviet Union. He had been in the right place at the right time, having the confidence to build on opportunities the new Russian State presented to those who were willing to seize them, take risks, and more importantly, who had the right connections. As a successful property developer with numerous international businesses, Rupert recognised few impediments to his commercial, entrepreneurial and private ambitions. Many of his actions were less than kosher, and he saw no barriers to applying these questionable business practices to Igor's personal ones.

According to Rupert, a man's pursuit of love needed a business plan, like those taught in the best business schools across the world. All Igor needed to do was develop a plan, research it, exercise it, and Daphne would be his. Rupert would apply a well-worked model — SWOT Analysis — and outline the Strengths, Weaknesses, Opportunities and Threats to Igor's situation, decide how to address the risks and implement the plan. Rupert made it sound plausible, scientific, methodical and quite easy.

In Rupert's analysis, Igor displayed considerable strengths: he was a good-looking, affluent, successful, personable man with a great deal of charisma. There were few weaknesses to his character. Currently, the barrier to obtaining the object of his desire was the threat of the husband. Once this threat was addressed, and removed, the opportunity could be snatched. It was that simple.

Igor started to relax, having enjoyed the academic encounter, as Rupert returned to the buffet for more fish and champagne. For the first time in days, he saw his situation was not terminal. There was some hope. He enjoyed Rupert's unguided enthusiasm and the way he seemed to embrace the unconventional challenge. Igor's melancholy state changed in a matter of minutes, thanks to his flamboyant school friend, and he could easily appreciate the merits of the suggested plan. Daphne's North American home, marital status, and commitment to her children did not pose the insurmountable problem Igor imagined, although the methods Rupert suggested were anything but orthodox.

In Rupert's analysis, the biggest problem for Igor was the spouse — Kevin. Once this impediment, or to use SWOT analysis, 'threat' was addressed, life could move on. Therefore, all Igor needed to do was remove Kevin from the equation. It was like attempting to build a property on a site subject to flooding: address the flooding problem and the problem is resolved. Rupert drew on numerous examples, where he worked, regarding the building of apartment blocks, hotels, bridges and ski resorts, and where there was an individual or physical impediment (threat) preventing the development. The removal of these individuals, or the situation, solved the issues and Rupert's empire had grown. Kevin needed to be removed. The solution was simple.

Rupert was clearly enjoying the hypothetical discussion, and the whole intellectual exercise. What had started as a day where he would have to feign interest in sporting events he could not fully appreciate was rapidly developing into an exciting project, requiring detailed planning, involving the discussion of many intricate, elaborate elements. He suggested that Igor befriend Kevin, invite him to Sochi, whereupon it would be relatively easy to arrange a fatal 'accident'. Igor had already explained that Kevin worked as a real estate lawyer in Vancouver. Igor and his company needed to show interest in acquiring properties in Vancouver and secure Kevin and his firm to act on their behalf. Once this relationship was established, Igor would invite Kevin, and maybe his colleagues, to Sochi to look at the hotels currently under construction for the 2014 Olympics. At this time, something could 'happen' to Kevin. Daphne would not be implicated and would remain totally innocent.

Listening to Rupert, it all appeared facile and plausible. Igor did not dwell on the ethical, moral or legal implications. He did not view this as an illegal criminal act, seeing it just as a way to secure the object of his desires. He soon became aware he was consulting a man who was not talking hypothetically. Rupert was not discussing dreams or fantasies: Rupert was totally earnest in his plan having, no doubt, been party to similar schemes before. While Igor was cautious and questioning, Rupert was calm and rational. In Rupert's life, and within his social circle, similar occurrences happened all the time. It was the modern way to do business and succeed in the new Russia.

Rupert looked at his watch and then the buffet table, debating if there was time for more food before leaving. He reluctantly decided he must depart, reconfirming he had immensely enjoyed the morning and wanted to stay in touch. He then suddenly changed track and his manner and persona became serious and subdued. Gone was the confident, grinning, enthusiastic individual talking loudly and commanding the conversation. Instead, he lowered his voice, leaned in towards Igor and nervously started to tell of events in his past, events Igor had heard rumours about, but had no actual details of.

Speaking earnestly, he told of a time in his past when, like Igor, he had been very much in love but mistakenly let that love slip through his fingers. He confessed there was not a single day when he did not regret what happened, admitting the loss of this love was the reason he remained single and would stay single for the rest of his life. He had never been able to find another woman who would replace this first true love — Rosa. While others may look at him and see a man whose life was complete — he had numerous friends, considerable wealth, charisma and charm — this was a façade. His life was incomplete and would always remain so because he did not have the woman he loved. There could be no other. It was that simple. In losing this woman, he also lost his ability to foster close personal ties. His heart was cold. He had difficulty forming empathetic ties, and relationships with anyone were problematic as he was perpetually frightened to form a close bond, whereby he could subsequently be hurt, as Rosa had hurt him. He therefore hoped Igor would pursue Daphne, leaving no stone unturned, and not make the same mistake he had. If he did not, it would lead to a life of regret. Igor required the strength and commitment that Rupert did not possess twenty years ago. He needed a coach, psychologically, to support him and Rupert wanted to play that role. At this point, both recognised a new level of friendship had been reached. They embraced and said goodbye. It would be an encounter Igor would remember for the rest of his life.

Igor left the event, speaking to no one, and returned to his hotel. His mood had dramatically changed. There was no longer a feeling of hopelessness, a sense of loss and defeat. There was the seed of a concrete plan, which he would thrash out on his laptop in the bar, later that afternoon. The objective would have a timescale; it would not be executed haphazardly or in haste. To achieve its resolution, he needed to proceed in a methodological manner, in a cautious way. He required a focus to ensure this was the right thing to do. More importantly, he needed to justify his intended actions to commit a murder and be sure nothing could go wrong.

Returning to his hotel, he found a corner table in the bar, hiding himself behind the potted plants so as not to be disturbed. He was energised. The more he thought of it, the more he believed it could work and he would not be detected. He was already aware the real-estate market in Vancouver was buoyant. The demand for hotel rooms was strong from the rapidly growing tourism market, which had been promoted by the success at the 2010 Winter Olympics in showcasing the city to the world. He would go to Vancouver the following year, 2013, purchase a hotel for development to add to his portfolio, and contract Kevin's firm to oversee the legalities. With hotels already in Russia, Croatia, the UK and Italy, branching out to North America would not be questioned. It was an acute business move, and for him the next logical step. Later that year, he would invite Kevin to Sochi to see a selection of hotels he was already involved with. The plan was in place. All that remained was its execution.

Prior to being awarded the 2014 Winter Olympics, Sochi was a small resort town, with forty thousand inhabitants, favoured by Russian leaders and politicians. Known as the 'Russian Riviera', it was the warmest city to ever host a Winter Olympics, and the first Olympics to be held in Russia since the dissolution of the Soviet Union. In the space of a few years, Sochi was set to be transformed into a state-of-the-art sports venue with lavish hotels, newly constructed sports venues, railway development and road links, all made possible by a fast-paced construction schedule which relied on a large influx of immigrant workers. Igor had been working in the construction industry for over twenty years, and was well versed with the way business was undertaken in Russia. His company was constructing five hotels in Sochi. Rupert had shown him how this expertise could be used to meet his personal objectives.

Late in January 2013, Igor took a series of flights from Sochi to Moscow, then to London and on to Vancouver, having already initiated email discussions with Kevin's firm, informing them of the type of properties he was interested in. Through his contacts, Kevin secured ten site visits in the two-week period Igor would be in Canada. Igor made no attempt to contact Daphne. Despite thinking of her every hour of every day and reliving countless times the brief occasions they had spent together, he adhered to her wishes and resisted any desire to reach out and have some form of contact. Each evening he would go to bed thinking of her and through the frequently disturbed night, he would wake, turn over, and she would be the only thing on his mind. There existed an odd excitement that she was the reason for his dramatic actions but completely oblivious to what was taking place, to the thoughts which dominated his days, and to his total commitment to her. She had no idea she was loved to this extent. He was also a little nervous that if he did contact her, she would reject him again, and if he were honest with himself, he did not know if he could bear that. Circumstances needed to radically change before they could be together. It was his intention to deliver this change.

Vancouver in late January was cold, wet, grey and rainy. Igor had been informed, on numerous occasions, that the city benefitted from its location at the base of mountains, on the coast, and was breathtakingly beautiful. These snow-clad mountains could easily, he was told, be seen from the downtown core. The inclement weather meant this sight was not forthcoming until the sixth day of his stay. He met Kevin and his colleague, Ryan, on his first morning in Vancouver, expecting not to feel any attachment to either men, wanting to adopt a professional distance suitable for a business relationship, but found he liked them both, enjoyed their relaxed yet professional personae, admired their intelligence, and appreciated their obvious knowledge. It was a difficult situation that Igor could not understand nor make sense of. Could you form a bond with an individual who was the spouse of the women you obsessed over, and whom you wanted dead? He called Rupert for guidance. True to form, Rupert provided the counsel he sought. Igor needed to keep his eye on the prize, Rupert advised, and not be distracted by emotions. Rupert confirmed that Igor's actions, while stressful, were going to have not only definite emotional benefits but also considerable financial ones. Rupert hinted that if he needed a partner for his Vancouver hotel venture, or others, he would be willing to offer support, both financial and moral. He also reminded Igor of the numerous contacts he had in Sochi, who were involved in the construction of the new facilities needed for the 2014 Sochi Olympic Games. Igor thanked him but declined the offer. He needed to complete the Vancouver business venture alone.

Once the two weeks were over, Kevin made offers on Igor's behalf for two buildings. Both needed considerable work to be developed into the boutique hotels now in vogue which would command the required rents, but he was sure these could be obtained. On his final night, Kevin and Igor ate at a waterfront restaurant in central Vancouver. During their time together, Kevin never mentioned his domestic situation, spoke Daphne's name, nor mentioned he was married, had children, nor what his hobbies were, nor of his friends. He spoke only of business. He had obviously enjoyed his time with Igor but was resolute in keeping a professional distance between business and pleasure, and Igor asked no prying questions. At this time, no property had been purchased, but Igor was confident one would. At the end of the evening, as the two men recognised this was to be the last time they would spend time together, Igor extended his well-rehearsed invitation for Kevin to visit Sochi as his guest, and become acquainted with the hotels he had already developed. As expected, Kevin leapt at the opportunity. He would love to come. He never suggested bringing a colleague, or his wife, or his children, and Igor ensured the offer was directed only to Kevin. Kevin was a man who liked to act alone, and this business link with Igor was his baby, and if it proceeded as anticipated, could reap considerable kudos for him in his company. Igor had not questioned any of the invoices Kevin presented and paid promptly. There were no red flags. In Kevin's eyes, the relationship was solid.

Upon returning to Russia, Igor quickly found time to meet with Rupert, who was keen to see how what he saw as his idea was progressing. They met in a hotel bar owned by Igor, in Sochi, in the summer of 2013, six months prior to the Winter Olympics. The entire town was a construction site. Immigrants from Molvania, Ukraine, Turkey and Central Asia were employed in every element of the building sector and in numerous related support industries. Russia's fifty-billion-dollar Sochi Olympics required seventy thousand immigrant workers who toiled for several years to ensure the Games could take place. Allegations that these workers endured long hours, unpaid wages, overcrowded accommodation and had their passports and documentation confiscated were rife in the international media, but were only half-heartedly addressed by the International Olympic Committee (IOC), who were keen to support Sochi's development and the forthcoming Games. The Sochi Olympics grew to be the most expensive sporting event in history, and one of the most controversial.

While the original mandate of the Olympic Games was to showcase the world's greatest athletes and create international cooperation and understanding, in the twenty-first century, they increasingly became a venue whereby certain countries, who were perceived to have questionable political reputations, were accused of using it to showcase their countries' actual and imaginary changing politics (e.g., Beijing, China, Sochi, Russia). While sport was the objective, other agendas were at play.

Kevin had no interest in politics, nor the debate over Sochi as a venue for the 2014 Winter Olympic Games. He saw his trip as a fact-finding mission, extending his understanding of his client's needs and one of the exceedingly rare perks that his time as a lawyer awarded. Cast in a similar mould, Igor and Rupert's priority was the generation of income, and if this entailed a few cost-cutting measures in order to achieve the promised goods — over fifty new hotels had been promised to the IOC — then these actions would be taken. If these actions were morally questionable, involving cronyism and corruption, Igor and Rupert could justify them. The pursuit of profit and showcasing Sochi as an international dynamic city to the world's media, delivering the best Winter Olympic Games ever, was the ultimate, national, patriotic goal. If a few lives were compromised or lost in achieving this aim, then so be it.

Ever since school, Igor had admired Rupert's energy and optimism. Rupert illustrated none of the aloof, distant characteristics so many of his countrymen displayed. He was a maverick, but also honest and genuine in a refreshing way. He told the truth, cut to the chase and did not obsess on the minute detail. He saw the big picture, the ultimate goal. Rupert listened as Igor relayed the information about his trip to Vancouver, then suggested he would provide a tour to Kevin of three of Sochi's new Olympic hotels. Rupert was aware one of these buildings was having construction issues, most recently with the supplier of railings specified for the external balconies. The supplier who was awarded the contract failed to deliver, so as a matter of urgency it had been necessary to purchase an alternative product that many knew did not meet the required safety specifications. If anyone were to lean on these railings, they could easily fail.

A plan was developing. It seemed easy. Igor questioned why Rupert was so willing to help and be involved in an act of murder. He liked Rupert, knew him to be phenomenally successful and influential. Why would he risk his reputation? Why trouble himself with a small player like Igor and his love life? At the end of the evening, Igor plucked up the courage, posing the troubling questions. Rupert smiled, obviously expecting to be asked for his justification.

'Because I want a challenge," he stated, adding, 'I do not want to just be a boring, conventional fifty-year-old businessman. I want secrets, I want excitement, I want to be different.'

Igor nodded, readily accepting this reasoning. He had always known there to be two types of people in business: those who follow the rules, do not make waves, or challenge the status quo, and consequently do not move on, or if they do, do so at a glacial pace. Then there are those who step outside the box, take risks, want to add spice to the cocktail of their lives and the lives of others. Rupert was one of these people. Rupert then provided a deeper, more personal interpretation. He confessed that since losing Rosa, a life — anyone's life — did not hold the same reverence it once did. When she left, she took all his emotions, all his compassion, his empathy: all his feelings left with her, rendering him an empty vessel where nothing mattered any more. Consequently, he experienced little emotion now over any actions undertaken, sanctioned or forbidden, good or bad, legal or illegal. Concluding the conversation, he stressed that he wanted nothing from Igor other than his friendship, and to be appreciated and included. Igor then understood the anticipation of the act, the adrenalin it would create, and their relationship was all the payment needed.

Rupert suggested that Kevin be invited to Sochi a week before the Games were due to start, in late January 2014. This would be the time the town would be the most occupied in the last push to finalise the construction of the hotels, roads, rail links and venues that everyone knew were well behind schedule. Although over forty thousand law enforcement officers, including police, Russian armed forces personnel, and four hundred Cossacks in traditional uniforms were to be deployed, the friends realised these security forces would be preoccupied with terrorism threats, the protection of all the international dignitaries, the athletes, and anticipated civil disobedience protests, to want to comprehensively investigate the accidental death of a Canadian lawyer. Igor's commitment to win the love of Daphne was no longer his alone: Rupert had become his silent partner in crime. Igor had not sought an accomplice, but it felt good to share the responsibility. Rupert had become a good friend and a confidant. They agreed to stay in touch and meet again in Sochi at the end of the year.

Kevin arrived in Sochi on January 24th, 2014, two weeks prior to the start of the Games. When telling Daphne he was working away on business in Russia, she expressed no surprise, nor more than a passing interest. He often travelled but this tended to be in North America. She drew no link between her brief affair with a Russian national, eighteen months ago in London, and her husband's trip to Sochi. While she thought of Igor often, her brief, passionate liaison had been neatly stored away in a box in the back of her mind. This box was frequently opened, explored and relived, but it remained tightly locked. It was a space as special and unique to her as the ones which held memories of the birth of her children, a picnic on the banks of the Seine with her mother and sister, and a drunken evening with three wonderful women in Las Vegas. But it was just a memory. Regrettably, there was no future. It could not be dwelt upon. It was over, never to be resurrected.

Kevin arrived in Russia, severely jetlagged. As he left the Sochi Airport Customs Hall a short, stocky man with a long black coat and hat with flaps covering his ears held up a laminated card displaying Kevin's name. He nodded without smiling as Kevin walked towards him, reached for Kevin's case, then led the way to a stretch limousine with tinted windows, parked illegally in the area reserved for the emergency services, and opened the rear door. For a fleeting moment, Kevin wondered if he was about to be kidnapped, but after such a long series of flights, did not possess the energy to dwell on these thoughts, so instead sunk thankfully into the black leather seats. He tried to resist falling asleep in the car smelling of cheap furniture polish.

Thirty minutes later, the vehicle drew up in front of the Grand Hotel Rosa and the silent stocky driver opened the door for Kevin, retrieved the suitcase, joked with the concierge and, for the first time, smiled, indicating his task was now complete. It was five p.m., already dark, but the hotel was illuminated in an elaborate manner, accentuating the gold décor. The lobby was quiet. Kevin was led to the reception by the concierge where the receptionist, who spoke perfect English, addressed Kevin as if he was the hotel's only guest. She had clearly been well-briefed on his arrival. He wondered if every client received the same treatment or if he was in some way special, but, as with his thoughts about being kidnapped, his mind and body were too fatigued to dwell on this. A few minutes later, he entered his ninth-floor room and after quickly consuming three of the mini-bottles of vodka and a packet of peanuts from the fridge, went to bed. It was six thirty p.m.

Kevin woke at six a.m. The curtains were open, his suitcase untouched from where the porter left it. The telephone message was flashing and for the briefest moment he failed to remember where he was supposed to be. He adored this sensation. It reminded him of his teenage years and of going out with friends on a Saturday night, getting drunk, getting laid (if he was lucky), returning home and in an intoxicated stupor, falling into bed. The next morning, maybe the next afternoon, he would wake, unable to recall immediately what occurred a few hours previously. Then his memory would gradually return, and he would lie in a glow, reliving the yesterday. That was a time of youth, of no cares, no commitments; a time vastly different to the adult one he found himself in now. He reached for the phone and pressed the message button. The woman who answered spoke English and informed him that Mr Igor Rakanowski would meet him for breakfast at eight a.m. in the Tolstoy Lounge. Kevin thanked her and replaced the receiver, ready to start his Russian adventure.

The Tolstoy Lounge was not difficult to find as a huge oil painting of his most famous heroine, Anna Karenina, covered one of the walls. Her piercing blue eyes seemed to follow the diners to their tables, as if accusing the patrons for the tragic circumstances of her life. Kevin was drawn to the woman's image. He knew her story of betrayal, family conflicts and marriage very well, having studied it for a course he took on Russian literature during his undergraduate studies: it was one of his favourites. He saw Igor seated at a table with another man, each appearing more relaxed and less formal than the other diners. The men stood as Kevin approached. Igor introduced Rupert as an old school acquaintance and the owner of the hotel, who also had interests in the hospitality industry, and who had been kind enough to offer to show Kevin some of his properties during his brief stay in Sochi. Igor suggested, as it was Kevin's first day and he was obviously going to feel tired after his long journey, that after breakfast they would take a relaxing three to four-hour drive around Sochi, to the Black Sea resorts, and then to the mountains and skiing communities, so he could become acquainted with the area. They would then return him to his hotel to rest and meet again for dinner. The following day they would visit three of Igor's hotels.

Kevin liked the itinerary. He was impressed with Igor's organisational skills, attention to detail and precision, noting the cultural difference to North America, where everything seemed more relaxed. He was beginning to admire the Soviet way of conducting business, and particularly liked the consumption of alcohol, available throughout the day in copious amounts. This society was well disciplined, formal and precise, but it also knew how to relax. He appreciated what he saw.

In the preceding weeks, Rupert had suggested to Igor that the best time for Kevin to meet his demise would be towards the end of his stay. The three of them would visit the hotel with the construction issues, consume vodka over a late lunch, as it was clear Kevin appreciated this drink, then take him to the sixteenth floor of the hotel to the suite with faulty balcony railings. The construction workers would have left for the day and 'friends' of Rupert's would ensure that the substandard railings in the show suite were, in fact, that. Kevin would be encouraged to access the balcony, admire the view towards the ski hills and, if all proceeded as expected, plunge to his death, falling through several pine trees as he went.

The chosen date was February 1st, less than a week from the opening ceremonies. The accident would, both men felt assured, be completely hushed up as the Sochi Olympic Organising Committee would not want the death of a foreigner — let alone a prominent lawyer, who met his fate due to cost-cutting construction techniques already highlighted in the western media — to overshadow the precise promotional schedule carefully developed during the previous eighteen months. Nothing was going to rain on this parade, especially as controversial publicity concerning the rights of the LGBT athletes and journalists during the Games had been gaining traction recently. Potential bad publicity would be buried quickly, along with the unfortunate victim.

Kevin suspected nothing. Igor and Rupert were the perfect hosts, having developed a timetable for his days. Each morning, after breakfast, he was met by one of them and driven to various hotels, restaurants and train stations, even to the Olympic venues themselves, frequently meeting other men who seemed to command the same elite privileges as his friends. Despite travel restrictions around Sochi, dubbed by the media as the 'Ring of Fire', his hosts were always granted access to wherever they wanted to go. Each day, Kevin made contacts he anticipated could be lucrative for him and his firm in the future. Lunch was always provided in a formal hotel dining room, restaurant, or bar, where large quantities of seafood were ordered, and vodka or wine consumed. He returned to his hotel in the late afternoon, free to respond to the day's emails, work, sleep or go out by himself and explore Sochi, already on fire with anticipation of the imminent event, now only days away. Mostly, he stayed in his room, ordered room service, drank vodka, watched television and slept.

On 1st February 2014, six days before the official opening ceremony, Igor collected Kevin from his hotel at ten a.m., as he had on previous days. The agenda for the day was to drive out of town to a spa hotel in the mountains, which Igor described as the jewel in his crown. After spending a couple of hours exploring this gem, they would return to Sochi to meet Rupert at one of his hotels, near to completion, on the coast of the Black Sea. All proceeded according to plan.

As the car reached its destination, Kevin could see an army of construction workers and gardeners seemingly packed so closely, he marvelled that they were able to work. Rupert explained that these workers were employed for long hours to complete the Alexander, which would be accepting guests in three days. Despite the chaotic site, Rupert felt confident that all the two hundred and forty-five rooms and suites would be completed and received a reassurance from the contractor this would occur. There was no back-up plan. The hotel had to open as all the rooms were booked and paid for. Kevin tried to accept this explanation while watching a large granite figure of a mermaid and dolphin lowered into the centre of a fountain adjacent to the hotel's entrance. Any doubts he kept to himself. Everything else seen in his brief time in Russia functioned well, and each of his friends exuded an air of confidence which did not warrant questioning.

Igor drove to the main entrance, parked the car, handed the keys to the valet and led Kevin into the lobby. Despite the lack of hotel guests, the restaurants had been accepting diners for the last three months and all seemed remarkably busy on this cold Saturday. Igor explained that the Russian elite loved dining out, and the head chef had been 'stolen' from a Michelin star restaurant in Switzerland, adding that this 'theft' cost more than the entire construction costs of the restaurants and kitchens, but was well worth it as the man's reputation was legendry. At that point, Rupert arrived.

'I chose the Conservatory for dining today,' he said. 'It's light and, if you do not mind, I need to ensure there are no operational issues, so will be half-working.'

Igor and Kevin were led to a table where three black-waist-coated waiters with red bow ties were waiting to seat them. Large vodkas were delivered without any requests as four women at an adjacent table stared on. This would be a fine place to spend the next couple of hours, Kevin thought, as he sipped his drink, deliberating again whether he should inflate his professional fees, as clearly his client had capital, as did his friends.

The three suited men spent a jovial couple of hours discussing hotels, the forthcoming Olympics and the economic legacy it was hoped the event would leave on the region. Sochi was already crowded with athletes, tourists and security personnel. Neither host was a sports enthusiast, viewing this intrusion solely as a way to generate income and build their business empires. The Olympics, together with the funds injected into the economy once the Games were awarded, had increased their personal wealth considerably. Anyone observing the interaction and the cool personae of the two well-dressed Russian businessmen entertaining their foreign lawyer would not have been able to imagine what was planned.

Rupert excused himself at four thirty p.m., saying he needed to make sure the workmen had left the show suite, and that it was ready for them. He returned as they were finishing their fifth vodkas, and suggested the tour commenced. Igor explained to Kevin his ambitions to incorporate some of the designs in the Alexander to the boutique hotel purchased in Vancouver. The dining room was quiet now, but the hotel remained busy with employees diligently cleaning every surface to ensure the establishment would be ready to receive guests in a few days. After touring the lobby, business meeting rooms, conference rooms, administrative offices and kitchens, they took the elevator to the sixteenth floor.

The doors opened and the smell of paint and newly fitted carpets was apparent as they walked down the long, windowless, wide corridor. Rupert explained that this floor had thirty premium suites, all with a balcony and views of either the Black Sea or mountains. He stopped and opened door to suite 1607.

The three men entered the spacious room. Directly opposite them, patio doors led to the balcony. To the left was a king-sized bed, covered with over-stuffed pillows; to the right, two sofas, a flatscreen television, desk, fridge and bar. Kevin was obviously impressed, quipping that his friends obviously saved the best until last, but questioning whether such a space would be needed in the proposed Vancouver Hotel. Igor and Rupert shared a glance and a smile. Rupert casually walked to the patio doors, opened them, and suggested the real feature was the wonderful views of the ski hills which could be seen from the corner by leaning a little over the balcony. Igor stood back, not for the first time impressed by his friend's calm delivery but nervous. Extremely nervous. He started to have second thoughts but knew these were too late, and instead tried to focus on the object of his desire: Daphne. No matter how he tried to conjure up her image he could not. Should he stop this plan which had developed over the last year and which, until now, he had never questioned? Kevin walked to the balcony, and following Rupert's instruction, leaned on the edge, straining to see the lights of the ski hills. Nothing happened. Igor looked questioningly at Rupert, who he could see was also somewhat surprised. Kevin turned, his back to the view and remained leaning on the railings, conscious of the cool evening air, realising he had consumed a lot of alcohol in the preceding hours and should sit down. At this point, there was a large crack and on cue, the railing broke. Kevin struggled, attempting to fall forward to save himself as he looked desperately at Igor, who remained motionless. To Igor's surprise, Rupert lunged forward, and with a fist firmly placed on the lawyer's chest, confidently pushed him away. The unapologetic actions of a man without empathy or emotions; a man who had his heart broken so badly he cared for no one. Kevin screamed as his body fell from the balcony, audibly breaking the branches of pine trees as it fell to the ground below. Then there was silence.

Igor and Rupert gingerly looked over the broken railing. It was too dark to see anything.

'Do you think he's dead?' asked Igor, visibly shaking. Rupert nodded and calmly took out his phone from his jacket pocket, calling the head of security. With little concern in his voice, he informed them of the 'accident'. Without speaking, the two men left the suite, took the elevator to the lobby, then left the building to trudge through the undergrowth to the area where they believed Kevin had met his demise.

The police arrived within the hour, and Rupert explained a tragic accident had occurred. All agreed there would be no need for an inquiry as two reputable witnesses had willingly given statements of the incident, but the Canadian Embassy needed to be informed. That could be done tomorrow. The body would be removed that night. There was no justification to undertake more than the minimum of paperwork, as all agreed that the security services had enough on their agendas at the current time, with recent intelligence suggesting the feminist punk band, Pussy Riot, had plans to disrupt sanctioned events within the next few days. This unfortunate accident needed to be cleared up and forgotten about quickly, so that more important issues could be dealt with.

Igor and Rupert answered the police officers' questions, provided their contact information, the address of the Hotel Rosa, and the room number where Kevin had been residing. Then, after also subtly thanking the lead officer with a suitable cash payment, they returned to the bar in the lobby.

'How are you feeling?' asked Rupert, as two large vodkas were placed in front of them. Igor shrugged.

'I feel nothing,' he replied, surprised at the accuracy of his response. They drank their drinks in silence. Murder should not be this easy, thought Igor, although he knew that with this man, in this society, at this time and with the right connections, it was. After quickly finishing his drink, he excused himself and went home. That night, he slept well.

Gordon Sillitoe had been in Sochi for only four days when he was called in to see the Canadian Ambassador, Julian Pavka. He presumed his ultimate boss wanted to see him to provide a welcome, introduce himself and discuss his new, albeit temporary, role as part of the diplomatic staff tasked with providing support for the Canadian athletes, dignitaries and tourists in Sochi for the 2014 Winter Olympics. As a young, junior diplomat, yet to reach his thirtieth birthday, his three-year career, to date, had been limited to the Federal Government offices in Ottawa. He was therefore looking forward to his new role and getting his hands dirty. In contrast, Julian Pavka had an extensive diplomatic career spanning over thirty years. Having been in Moscow for almost a decade, the son of Russian immigrants who arrived in Canada in the 1940s, he spoke fluent Russian, and was well acquainted with the rapidly changing society and culture. He greeted Gordon in a large temporary office, and in a detached, measured voice, he explained there had been an accidental death of a Canadian lawyer and that Gordon was to complete the necessary paperwork, inform the next-of-kin, organise the repatriation of the body to Canada and, as a matter of urgency, clear the victim's hotel suite as it was needed for forthcoming Olympic guests. The meeting lasted less than five minutes. Julian Pavka explained that most of his diplomatic staff were already assigned to more pressing matters related to the Olympics which were, of course, only a matter of days away. He did not ask whether Gordon had any questions, or if he felt confident completing these tasks — this was automatically presumed. Gordon was given the contact details of the police officer in charge of the accident, the witnesses' names, and the address of the Hotel Rosa where the victim had been staying. Nothing else was needed. As an afterthought, Julian Pavka added, 'Welcome to Sochi', then picked up a paper on his desk, indicating the meeting was over.

Gordon left the room and immediately called Igor, arranging to see him an hour later at the hotel, impressed by how easy arranging this rendezvous was. They met, as planned, and Igor explained the situation and accompanied Gordon to the suite where Kevin had been staying. With little conversation, the two men emptied the wardrobe and drawers, placing clothes and toiletries in the victim's case. Gordon pondered if it would not have been better to throw everything away, thinking how emotionally devastating it would be for the family of this poor individual to receive these possessions, including a laundry bag of dirty underwear, socks and shirts, weeks after the death. At the Embassy, Gordon had been informed by one of the more senior diplomats that the timing of this death was highly inconvenient, as flights were overbooked because of the Olympics, even for cargo, so space for a coffin would not be easy to secure. This poor man's estate would be paying large sums if they wanted his body returned within the next month, and even if they did not, storage would be very costly.

Igor provided Gordon with the address of Kevin's law firm in Vancouver and thanked him for his assistance. Gordon assured him the Government of Canada was accustomed to dealing with the sudden deaths of its citizens while abroad. It even had a website just for the purpose of conveying this information to unfortunate relatives and would be dealing with everything in a professional and dignified manner. He felt very mature and accomplished in giving this information. Maybe this assignment was not as bad as originally thought. He asked Igor not to contact Kevin's employer for at least a week so they could be informed using the appropriate channels. Igor agreed. The two men exchanged business cards, thanked each other and said goodbye. This was to be Igor's last contact with the authorities in both Canada and Russia, confirming Rupert's information: it was possible to get away with murder in the new Russia: 'Hot, Cool, Yours.'

Arriving in his Vancouver office at nine thirty a.m. on Monday 3rd February, Peter Bailey — senior partner at Alexis, Bailey and Braithwaite — was greeted by a flustered legal clerk informing him that a police officer had been waiting to see him since eight thirty a.m. 'Does he have an appointment?' Peter asked, annoyed that his day was already about to be disrupted before it started. 'No, but he said it was a matter of great importance, and he has been waiting an hour,' his colleague responded. Peter sighed, asked if the conference room was being used and when learning it was not, stated he would meet the officer there in five minutes.

The plain-clothes police officer was already seated, coffee in hand, admiring the Vancouver skyline from the twentieth-floor office when Peter entered. He stood up, looking tense, while numerous thoughts raced around Peter's mind. In Peter's experience, unannounced visits from police officers seldom bore good news. 'Peter Bailey — how can I help you?' Peter said, confidently holding out his hand. After shaking the outstretched hand and introducing himself, Alan Wakeman nervously started to explain what had happened to Peter's colleague in Sochi: a tragic accident, which he thought it better to inform Peter about before conveying the news to the family. Peter sat down, obviously shocked but agreeing this to be the best option. He explained while he was not close to Kevin, adding that no one really was, Kevin was a very competent lawyer, and certainly managed to attract some extremely high fees from well-respected clients. His leads in Sochi were such clients and represented a growth area for the firm.

Alan Wakeman nodded his head in agreement and then stood up, wanting to leave the situation as soon as possible. He explained his role was to inform the next of kin, but the logistics of transporting the body back to Canada were with the Canadian Consulate in Sochi, adding they were currently under a lot of stress and increased workload because of the Winter Olympics. He gave Peter their contact information and then asked if he would like to accompany him to inform Peter's wife, Daphne, of the accident. Peter could tell the officer wished this to occur so agreed, confirming he would be ready to leave in an hour, after rescheduling his day, cancelling a couple of meetings and informing his staff.

Peter had only been to Kevin's house on one previous occasion, many years ago, and knew Daphne very slightly, primarily from office Christmas parties. He had no idea if she would be at home on a cold, dreary February morning. The two men made polite conversation during the forty-minute drive. Peter explained that Kevin had been working with some Russian clients on the acquisition of hotels in Vancouver and been invited to Sochi to see similar ventures. He knew little of Kevin's work or clients, adding that Kevin was a competent lawyer who did not need supervising.

As they approached the neat, large, suburban house, it appeared unoccupied. Neither men relished the thought of holding on to the news, which the spouse was unaware of, any longer than necessary. If Daphne were not at home, Peter would have no suggestions where she could be. They rang the doorbell and heard movement. Daphne answered, dressed in track pants, obviously having just returned from a run; a welcoming smile on her face. Her expression changed as she saw Peter accompanied by a formally dressed stranger. 'Hi,

Daphne. This is Alan Wakeman. He is a policeman. We need to come in and talk to you.' Peter's words sounded clumsy.

'Of course,' she said and led the way to the open-plan kitchen, gesturing they be seated on the kitchen stools. 'Can I get you anything? Tea, coffee, water? Excuse my attire, I've just come back from a run and it started to rain, so I'm a bit bedraggled.'

She stammered a little, and spoke fast, obviously worried about what she was going to hear. Peter declined for them both and considered if he should ask Daphne to sit down, or if he should try to hold her hand, but realised such intimacy was inappropriate as he really did not know her that well.

Alan Wakeman seemed reluctant to speak, leading Peter to question his presence. After a brief, odd silence, Peter took the lead, calmly explaining what had happened. Daphne sat down, played with her wedding ring, and expressed no emotion as he documented what he understood had occurred. It was not until he mentioned that Kevin was in Sochi with a new client, Igor Rakanowski, did she gasp and appear visibly shaken.

'How did they meet?' she asked, and Peter explained about the hotel developments in Vancouver. The police officer remained silent, forgotten in the drama. Daphne got up and started to pace around the kitchen. She was not crying but shaking, shocked; asking questions in a random way. How would his body be returned home? Where was it now? Where were his things? How would she tell the children? What would happen to all his work? What about his income — would there be enough for the school fees? Then she broke down and Peter knew he could now hold her and provide the physical comfort that was totally appropriate. He was quick to explain that the firm would be there to provide every support she needed and if she wanted, he could liaise with the Canadian diplomats in Russia and Canada tasked to deal with the accident. She looked relieved and thanked him, immediately agreeing to this offer. Alan Wakeman added that his Victim Support Unit was excellent at these times, and he could easily arrange for someone to contact her. Daphne declined this approach, confirming that she had incredibly close girlfriends whom she could call on, which is what she intended to do the moment they went. With this prompt, they left, both relieved but stressing that they would be contacting her the following day.

Daphne watched their car drive away. She was numb. Everything she wanted for years delivered in one small element of time. There was so much to think about, most importantly the children, all away at boarding school. But they could wait. She would tell them in person in a few days — on Friday, so they could return home and be with her to grieve and adjust. At this time what she needed most was the counsel of Andrea and Kate. She called both in turn and while not disclosing her news, asked that they visit her that evening after they finished work. They agreed. Daphne had never made such a demand before: it must be important.

She was left alone. The rest of the world turned in an established way, but her life would never be the same again. Thank goodness. Her husband, whom she did not love, who was cruel, alcoholic and violent, was dead. He had been working, unbeknown to her, with a Russian man she knew slightly and who, in another life, conveyed his deep, sincere love for her. Kevin had been killed in a foreign land by accident, when her lover was present, and there seemed to be no doubt in anyone's mind it was anything but an unfortunate accident. Anyone's mind, except hers.

Kate and Daphne arrived at seven p.m., bottles of wine in hand, knocked on Daphne's door and let themselves in, as true friends would. Daphne was in the kitchen; a plate of olives and feta cheese and sushi she ordered an hour ago on the kitchen island, untouched. Her eyes were red and she was wearing yoga attire. Despite obviously making little effort, she still looked good, thought Andrea.

'So, what's all this about?' asked Kate, taking off her jacket and shoes, showing no hesitation in cutting to the chase. Daphne found glasses and started to pour wine from a bottle, already half-empty, and proceeded to tell them of the events of the day, and her new-found status as widow, as her friends sat and silently listened.

'Oh my God!' exclaimed Kate. 'Your lover has murdered your husband: it's almost nineteenth century romantic novel material. Are you going to tell anyone?' Daphne explained that, upon reflection, Igor had done her a huge favour. For the first time in decades, she felt free, could do what she wanted and was not afraid for herself or her children. She knew it was murder but if she did choose to report it to the Canadian authorities, there was little they could do. The Russians had already covered it up. Igor had a lot of friends in influential places. It had to be accepted, which is the conclusion she reached after a day reflecting on the options.

They raised their glasses to this decision.

"Have you heard from Igor?" asked Andrea. Daphne explained there had been no contact since she last saw him in London, eighteen months ago. She went on to tell them how very upset he was when she told him there could be no future, but she thought he would get over her, and he was just being melodramatic in his insistence of undying love. She explained that she thought it a bit disconcerting when he said he would not give her up and would always hope to be her 'man of the future'.

'Clearly, he did not get over you, did he?' Andrea added, reaching for a piece of California roll.

The following month, Kevin's law firm organised the memorial service for their partner, with Daphne's input. She was grateful for this, finding it difficult to think of nice things to say about the man she hated. Far better that others do it. Kevin's legal colleagues were perfect in accommodating the wishes of a grieving spouse, seeing nothing wrong when she declined to speak on the occasion.

As the weeks following the memorial passed, thoughts of Igor became more prevalent. Daphne knew he would contact her but could not predict if this would be next week, next month or next year. In May, two months after the memorial morning, when she was home alone, deciding whether to go for a run or clean the fridge, she answered the door and found him standing in front of her, a large bunch of red roses in hand, formally dressed in dark suit and tie, looking extremely nervous, but incredibly sexy.

'I was waiting for this day,' she said, opening the door and granting him access, letting him kiss her on the cheek as he did so.

In anticipating the encounter, she was well prepared in her mind concerning how it would proceed. She knew exactly what she wanted. She knew exactly what she did not want. All options were rehearsed well, in her mind, during the long nights of wakefulness since Kevin's death. After twenty years in an abusive, loveless, threatening relationship, she could not consider sharing her life so totally with any man ever again. And as always, her children came first, at least for the next few years. But she did crave physical contact, and when she thought of Igor, it tended to be the most intense, physical times her mind was drawn to. In over fifty years she had had sex with only two men: Kevin and Igor. She loathed sex with Kevin, which had become violent, hurtful and devoid of any affection, contrasting sharply with the wonderful, tender, physically playful intimacy she shared on the few occasions with Igor. A few years ago, she heard an interview with the film director and actor, Woody Allen. He had been asked what his biggest regret was now, in his sixties, and replied, 'Not enough sex.' She felt the same. Totally unaware of what 'enough sex' would involve, she knew she wanted to pursue this goal. She wanted more sex.

Her life had changed for the better and she did not want to ever go back. She had a comfortable income: Kevin's life insurance paid out well. There were few debts, her children — while not perfect — were, for the most part, good kids and she had wonderful girlfriends. She was resolute that no man should upset this. Igor would be welcome in her life, but on her terms. These terms she articulated as he sat drinking herbal tea at her kitchen island, a huge grin on his face and tears in his eyes. He accepted them without question, adding that he would be spending time between his hotels in Sochi, London, Milan and Vancouver. Kevin's death was not discussed. Daphne's new life was born.

Chapter 5
United by Emotion
Tokyo, Summer Olympics 2021

Like so many elements in the women's lives, the decision to celebrate their sixtieth birthday year, 2019, in Japan was more to do with circumstances and fate than a passionate desire to see this exotic Eastern country, and in no small way influenced by the forthcoming 2020 Summer Olympic Games.

In 2013, Japan was awarded the 2020 Summer Olympics, beating rival bids from Istanbul and Madrid. Over the recent past, many cities had been reluctant to host the event, citing issues of security and costs. This was not the case in Japan. Earlier in the year, a poll showed that seventy-three per cent of the residents of Tokyo supported the bid. The I.O.C. particularly favoured the fact that eighty-five per cent of events would be within eight kilometres of the Olympic Village in Tokyo, making these Games compact. Japan was also perceived to be a very safe venue. These Games were well supported: two hundred and four thousand applicants from around the world were received by individuals who wanted to volunteer.

Eighty thousand were recruited. The country was immensely proud to be hosting the event.

Following Jo's company's success with their involvement at previous Olympics, especially in Vancouver, London and Sochi, Bernard Trim, the owner of Holden Sealants, was enthusiastic to have a large presence in Tokyo. While sales of his sealant to the Japanese market had been slowly growing over the last decade, this had been at a glacial pace: the country remained a tough nut to crack. The Japanese population had the reputation of being suspicious of products not sourced internally. This patriotic, cultural commitment to buy locally manufactured goods was not unique to sealant: it was well known amongst international companies who sought to enter this distinctive Asian market. Bernard saw Japan as an exciting challenge — and he loved a challenge, especially in this case, where the efforts, if successful, would be worth the hard work, as the Japanese also had the reputation of being good, reliable customers. Once they committed to a product or brand, they remained loyal. The 2020 Olympics and Holden Sealants' promotional activities during this event was seen to be the push needed. Bernard suggested that, prior to the Olympics, Jo visit Tokyo, speak to their existing customers and the sales representatives they had in place, ascertain what was required to stimulate sales and develop a marketing plan. She was tasked to explore venues for receptions and parties during the 2020 Olympics, and deliver a detailed document, complete with budgetary projections to build on existing sales and generate significant new ones. As ever, she was up to the challenge.

It had been over ten years since Kate became involved with the security issues surrounding the Canadian athletes, dignitaries and tourists attending the Games in Vancouver. She had utilised this experience dealing with four subsequent Olympic venues (London, Sochi, Rio de Janeiro and Pyeongchang), which meant she was now seen as the RCMP's Olympic Games expert. Although eligible to retire with a good pension, she was persuaded to remain with the organisation until after the 2020 Tokyo Olympics and agreed without hesitation. She liked her work, enjoyed being busy and was unsure how she would fill her days, once retired. It had not been a hard decision to stay. In overseeing the Canadian law enforcements' activities in Japan, she was required to take a couple of trips to liaise with the Canadian Embassy in Tokyo and her Japanese law enforcement counterparts prior to 2020. These visits could be undertaken at Kate's discretion. During the summer of 2019, she called Jo, knowing there would be a good chance she would also be in Japan, prior to the 2020 Summer Games, and suggested they celebrate their sixtieth year in Tokyo with Daphne and Andrea. Jo agreed, adding they should make it a two-city vacation and spend a few days in Tokyo and then take the famous bullet train to the historic city of Kyoto.

Their sixtieth-year birthday celebration was a given. With Jo and Kate's work commitments, funding the get-together was not an issue for them. Daphne had a significant income, so the trip would not cause her any financial hardship. It was only Andrea who, as a nurse, did not have large reserves and might find the cost preventative, but upon learning of the proposal she had no hesitation. Andrea's maternal grandparents were Japanese: consequently, she had always held a deep affection and fascination for the country and its culture and had long wanted to visit, but never, until now, been given the opportunity. She would not miss it for the world!

Daphne offered to share a suite with Andrea, saying she would cover the cost of the accommodation providing she had first choice of bed and was not pestered to exit the bathroom, no matter how long she spent in there. Andrea happily agreed, and with arrangements sorted, the holiday was planned for the last week of October 2019.

Jo and Kate undertook their work commitments in Japan, prior to Daphne and Andrea's arrival, enabling them to get acquainted with the city, the intricate train system, the subway, the sheer volume of people moving across the streets, the amazing shopping centres and food courts offering every sort of cuisine, and a few good (and bad) restaurants. They all booked the same hotel; a centrally located, western-style one with spa, that Jo found, for their vacation time.

The women had not been together since a few days in 2016, when Jo paid a fleeting visit to Vancouver. This week was, therefore, very special, similar to the one they spent for their fortieth birthday year in New York City and their fiftieth in Las Vegas. With considerable anticipation and excitement, they all saw it as the highpoint of their year. While there were emails and telephone calls in the intervening years, these forms of contact could never replace sitting around late in the evening, drinking wine and sharing confidences no one else knew of. A lot had happened in their respective lives; a lot which could only be shared and discussed face to face — something they all recognised.

Andrea told Peter of the holiday the day she booked her flight. It was dinner time and he had made pasta with a seafood sauce and garlic-herb bread, which she was trying (unsuccessfully) to resist. As they were eating, she excitedly explained the plans that were already in place, the happiness she felt being with her best friends and, at long last, visiting the country of her grandparents' birth. He listened but was quiet, offering no comments and asking no questions. The silence was unsettling. She had expected him to be happy and supportive, like he generally was to the events in her life: not quiet, sullen and unresponsive. With her frustration growing, she eventually stood up, demanding to know if he was jealous, seeing no other reason for his silent state. He had finished his food as she had barely touched hers. Replacing cutlery, he calmly said he was not jealous, adding, 'It's just that I planned we would go together.' He then went on to gently explain he had been asked to be the physiotherapist for the Canadian Olympic Men's Field Hockey Team during their 2020 trip and had, of course, said yes. As a surprise, he had purchased flights and arranged hotels so they could both go together, knowing how much she wanted to visit. It was going to be a special gift to celebrate her sixtieth birthday.

Andrea smiled broadly, as tears welled up in her eyes. Despite everything, all the ups and downs, all the secrets and the lies told over the years, which they were both guilty of, he really was one of the sweetest, most generous and sensitive men she had ever known. Again, the nagging doubts, which were becoming increasingly common, over her relationship with Brad surfaced in her consciousness, as she put her arms around Peter's neck and tussled his hair. She then hastily explained a holiday with her three best girlfriends was entirely different to a holiday with her spouse, especially as that holiday with him would include the Olympic Games, and hopefully, a trip to the birthplace of her grandparents. They were two unique, distinct events. With her girlfriends there would be a lot of eating, drinking, shopping, laughing and gossiping with the venue being secondary to the girlfriend bonding. With him, there would be the Games as well as sightseeing and exploring the culture. Although in the same country, both holidays were totally different: both would be very special.

Peter relaxed, accepted the reasoning and started to ask questions, in a genuinely interested way, on the logistics of her trip, where they would all be staying and how they would travel within the country. Andrea answered but her mind was wandering as she thought of how she would tell Brad not only of the holiday, but of the end of their affair.

For the last five years Andrea had been leading a double life, which no one she believed suspected. Seeing Brad at Vancouver Airport in 2009 did not cause an earthquake in her existence, but it did seriously disrupt her equilibrium. It was not until Amy's sixteenth birthday, 12th May 2015, six years after seeing him again, that she had the courage to telephone the hardware store in her hometown, and speak to him. For the next year, their relationship consisted solely of telephone calls and, upon her insistence, contact was always initiated by her. At first, these conversations involved the required catching-up, necessitated by twenty years apart, but soon grew longer, more flirtatious and eventually amorous. Texting her frequently, he would send brief sentiments such as 'Missing you', or quote lyrics to songs from their past; words she read and reread throughout the day, but was always careful to delete when returning home. In May

2016, after much anticipation and careful thought, Brad made the seven-hundred-kilometre trip to see her for a weekend: their first face-to-face date. They met in a hotel on the outskirts of Vancouver, Andrea not wanting to risk meeting anywhere where she could see someone she knew. There was no time in her life she was not more apprehensive and scared, nor more excited. In the months prior to the meeting, it seemed as if her whole persona changed, inwardly and outwardly. Colleagues kept telling her she looked good; total strangers smiled at her in the street; she spent a couple of hours each night awake, fantasising about their first meeting; she had an inner glow and lost seven pounds in weight with no dieting or effort. She was a new person, with more energy and zest, all attributed to him. She found herself consistently happy, optimistic and positive, no matter what life threw at her. Brad was her big secret. She confided only to Daphne, sometimes speaking to her two or three times a day, there being no one else to share her excitement. Daphne did not mind, delighted for her friend who was the happiest she had ever known her, knowing this supportive role was needed. The secret was better not shared extensively.

Daphne advised not sleeping with Brad on the first date, drawing on information she learned overhearing girls talk at high-school, which had not been up-dated, and which she had not followed herself. She believed 'nice girls' did not do this, and Andrea was a nice girl. Daphne told her to buy expensive, distinctive perfume, so Brad would have a lasting aroma to remind him of her, and to wear clothes she felt good in, but to resist buying expensive new outfits that could announce the indiscretion to Peter or Amy. Andrea was not at all concerned about Peter, who lived his own life, had secrets of his own and had no interest in her attire. Likewise, Amy was a teenage girl too preoccupied with her own life to have more than a passing interest in her mother's activities.

The first few weekends they spent together were just as anticipated: wonderful and exciting. She did not follow her friend's advice concerning delaying sex, although she intended to. But after almost thirty years of wanting him, how could she? She realised the things she had been dreading and dwelling on during the nights thinking about the logistics of their first sexual encounter — things such as the embarrassment of appearing naked in front of him for the first time, going to the bathroom in a hotel room which may not have the best soundproofing, what underwear to wear, and how uncomfortable all that lace would be next to her skin — were not as stressful as imagined. The couple quickly developed an understanding and acceptance of each other, and each other's bodies. Everything, at first, was perfect.

The relationship therefore reached its sexual phase in 2016 in a non-descript, functional hotel room by Vancouver airport, where Brad stayed during visits. Andrea had only had one previous sexual partner —

Peter — and there had been very few occasions when they shared any sexual intimacy. Initially there had been infrequent physical contact, but not for almost two decades. She soon realised Brad's experience was considerably greater than hers. He had no inhibitions and while, for the most part, she did find the sex enjoyable, it was only that — never fantastic. She was never left screaming for more, nor wanting the experience to be repeated as soon as possible. It was always over quickly, with little fore or after play, no matter how often she tried to influence this to address her desires. It was never as romantic, nor as tender, as she thought it should be. Despite the numerous subtle clues she felt she gave, the positions they adopted, the words spoken, or the time they had together, there was perpetually something missing. Good, but never great. Why? Her sentiments, she knew, mirrored those of women who had the same sexual partner for years, and should not, she rationalised, be those of a woman who had only been offered the mouth-watering fruit recently, after having been denied it all her life. She questioned if something was wrong with her.

As they spent more and more time together — always during weekends when he could come to Vancouver — she developed what she reluctantly recognised to be nagging doubts, difficult to rationalise. There were little things that made her apprehensive and question her affection towards him. The man she had been so much in love with, who dramatically departed from her life, changed her destiny, only to reappear, was proving not to live up to her expectations. He was her first true love: his re-entry into her life meant it should now all be perfect. But it was not.

After a while, it seemed that every time they met, he said something, or did something, which made her uneasy. One of the first times was when discussing his two daughters, now adults, and living in Eastern Canada. He described seeing them only once a year throughout their adolescent years, for two weeks in August, and then when they turned eighteen, curtailing even this brief interaction. Andrea could not believe anyone would not want to see their children and take an active part in that child's life and development. She could never in her wildest dreams imagine not seeing Amy. But Brad had little contact, and did not apologise for this, seeming to think it unexceptional. Andrea also suspected he paid no maintenance to Kathy, his wife, although was not brave enough to ask him outright.

He also had the habit of commenting on her appearance in an almost sexist way. He spoke often of her clothes and dress sense, saying things such as, 'Can you wear a shorter skirt next time we meet, as I like looking at your legs,' and 'I think I would like you better if you cut your hair shorter and tidied it up,' and the most hurtful comment, 'That necklace (the one Amy bought her) looks really cheap.' While not pervasive, these comments were building: little clues nagging at her consciousness, suggesting things were not as perfect as she wanted them to be.

She sheepishly conveyed her reservations to Daphne. It felt totally wrong to have wanted someone so long, to have been so besotted, to have all these fantasies for such a long time, only to then spend an inaudible amount of time focusing on his faults. As time progressed, things did not improve as she hoped they would and if anything, got worse. She no longer wanted to sleep with him or talk to him, and had no intention of building a life with him as originally planned. She wanted things to improve and kept thinking they would, but eventually, reluctantly, conceded they would not. Aware that she was doing neither of them any favours in prolonging the affair, she accepted she needed to tell him this relationship was over. This would be her first break-up. Sixty-years old and ditching a man for the first time. Meeting her best friends in Japan would enable her to seek their counsel, discuss the options and determine the best way it could be ensured with the least amount of pain. She needed their advice and looked forward to the time when she was able to tell them of the thoughts dominating her days. She did not want to hurt Brad but needed to end the relationship as there was now nothing left. Her friends would know how.

The sixtieth-birthday celebration week was everything they each anticipated. While the weather was not accommodating and the restaurants more expensive than expected, the bonding was superb as, over the course of eight days, each woman gave up-dates of her life.

The first four days in Tokyo were spent exploring the busy streets and getting lost on numerous occasions. Unlike so many other tourist towns across the world, there were few instructions in English and at the end of the first day, when a great deal of time had been spent walking, debating and arguing, trying to find the famous fish market, the fashion sector, and the Imperial Palace, they decided that to preserve their relationship they needed to investigate organised tours, so the remaining days would not be wasted, and their friendship would survive. That evening, they sat in the hotel's bar, drank Japanese beers, ate hotel food, and booked full-day tours to Mount Fuji and the Imperial Palace. Daphne was keen to spend an evening experiencing the sumo wrestling demonstration followed by a traditional Japanese meal, but the others showed no enthusiasm, stating they were not interested in watching fat, sweaty men throw each other around and grunt. Instead, they all registered for an evening's sushi-making class, agreeing it to be more suitable for women of their age.

After four days in Tokyo, they took the bullet train to Kyoto, a smaller city undamaged by any wars, with picturesque small, winding roads and historical alleyways. The highlight of their four days here was to be a 'Kimono Experience', which Daphne had read about, and the others reluctantly agreed to, having denied her the sumo wrestling demonstration.

The taxi arrived to collect them at their hotel at nine a.m., driving them through a maze of narrow lanes and alleyways to a small boutique in the old part of town. Here, each selected a kimono to wear, complete with the traditional obi (sash), shoes and bag. Finding a kimono for Kate was especially challenging because of her height, while Daphne wanted to try almost every one on offer, eventually deciding to pay a little more for the genuine silk, vintage article. The Japanese women employed at the boutique applied traditional make-up, transforming them to look like geisha women, going on to style their hair with numerous accessories required to keep it in place. The entire, elaborate transformation process took over an hour. Upon leaving the boutique in the new disguises, the four explored the streets, giggling, tripping over while attempting to walk in the tight long skirts, stopping to take numerous photographs and encountering other tourists who had obviously also decided to indulge in the same cultural experience. The day was unique, never to be forgotten by any of them. 'The best experience ever!' beamed Andrea, who they all agreed looked the best in her peach-coloured robe.

Their time in Kyoto also included excursions to the Kinkaku-ji temple and Fushimi Inari-taisha shrine. By the end of the holiday, they had lost count how many temples and shrines they had seen, where they were and what they were all called. The culture and society were unlike any they encountered before. Daphne wondered if they should not repeat the experience the following year, as Kate, Jo and Andrea were all to be at the 2020 Summer Olympics in Tokyo, but Kate and Jo were quick to confirm their time then would be for working, not dressing up, and Andrea added she had promised to be with Peter and to see the Olympics with him.

During their time together, each provided updates on their lives and loves. Kate enthused over her work and the life of a single girl, stating that there were a couple of men in her life, who she saw on an almost regular basis, on her terms, and who provided all the flirtation and affection she needed. One was married, and although she did feel some pangs of guilt over this primarily sexual liaison, she was able to rationalise it: he was not interested in leaving his wife or family; it was just fun and convenient for the two of them. Despite it being almost ten years since Bob's death, she was resolute there could be no replacement, and would never admit another man into her life full-time. Confessing the first few years alone had been difficult, she now enjoyed her work and was good at it; she had gained a respect amongst her colleagues and established a comfortable routine, which — while challenging — she could address. She had a confidence never known when younger, rarely got stressed or nervous, and surprisingly liked being an 'older' woman much more than being a younger one.

Jo concurred that she also had an inner confidence, elusive thirty years ago. She then went on to tell them about the new love in her life — Rachel. Upon hearing this news, everyone's jaw dropped, as Andrea asked the obvious question.

'Is Rachel a woman?'

Rachel was indeed a woman, and an increasingly important one in Jo's life. A retired teacher, they met three years ago at a pottery class, then — as Jo uneasily explained — became good friends and then lovers. She added that Rachel had two teenage daughters who accepted her, and whom she really liked. They were now discussing living together as a family. In recognising the expressions of her listeners, Jo quickly confirmed that Rachel would never replace the bond she had with the three of them, but needed their understanding and support as, for the first time in her life, she felt she knew herself, could be herself and was very, very content. Looking directly at Kate when describing this new-found state, she was rewarded with Kate's broad smile: her best friend confirming they were all delighted for her. Daphne, looking more than a little perplexed, added that there were hundreds of questions racing around her head about the nature of lesbian relations; questions she had harboured for years, ever since learning there were such things as lesbian relationships when at high school, but was not brave enough to pose, or go online to find the answers. It was such good news that, at long last, she had a 'go-to' person to approach. Jo smiled, adding that although her admission may seem revolutionary, there were a number of women — and men — who, after a long-term heterosexual relationship, 'move on' to a homosexual one later in life, suggesting this may not be the right time to provide detailed answers to all Daphne's enquiries.

'I love the way, as a group, we never fail to introduce new topics and issues to generate excitement,' added Kate, happy to leave the discussion of lesbian intimacy for another occasion.

Daphne gave a report of her children, all now at various universities, and her relationship with Igor, describing it as perfect for her. She saw him between four and six times a year, with at least a couple of these occasions being in Vancouver, but not when her children were in town. The other occasions would be for a week or more in either London, Milan or Sochi — the cities where he owned hotels. It suited them both very well. Like Kate, she confessed, she would never want him as a live-in-lover, cherishing her independence too much. On the occasions she felt in need of company (or sex), he was always there for her. Kate asked if Kevin was ever mentioned. He was not, and when Daphne did forget herself and said something like, 'That's the sort of thing my husband would do,' she felt an immediate tension and was at pains to erase the faux pas. Kevin would always be the elephant in the room: never completely forgotten, but easily possible to ignore.

Andrea had always been the quietest of the group, slower to share, but consistently an avid listener and sage advisor. It took a few days in Japan, and a few glasses of wine, before she had the confidence to tell Kate and Jo the circumstances of her life that Daphne already knew of. When she did, it was with relief, as she explained to them how strange the process of welcoming Brad back into her life had been. It had been slow and cautious, and progressed from extreme excitement to almost dread. After many years, she felt sure he was not what she wanted, and could never be, and this seemed bizarre as for the longest time, she thought he was all she desired. Peter was not perfect, and as everyone knew, told her he was gay many years ago. They had been living together as friends — good friends — without any physical contact, but with a great rapport and deep appreciation of each other. She had loved Brad, or thought she did, when she was a young woman, when she was in a different location, when she was naive and inexperienced. It had been foolish to think this intense, adolescent love could be rekindled thirty years later, when they each had changed so much, when they lived in different places and had such different life experiences. She concluded that she would be finishing the relationship soon, if brave enough, but did not know how, as initially she provided so much encouragement to him and was now feeling guilty because of this. She did not want to hurt him but was unsure how not to. Her friends confirmed that this hurt was inevitable and she needed to tell him as soon as possible.

In attempting to ease Andrea's concern, Kate offered one of her own personal experiences — something not shared with the group before — but in so doing presented an interpretation suggesting everyone had a 'Brad' in their past. She described this person as 'TOTGA' — The One That Got Away. To elaborate her point, she then told of Doug, a boy known in high-school, who was her first teenage love infatuation when she was sixteen. They never dated, but flirted extensively, kissed on one occasion behind the science block, got on exceptionally well, did school projects together, shared the same sense of humour and had many similarities. They had a real, inexplicable connection. He was tall, his father was also a police officer, and like her, had younger siblings. He was the first boy to describe her as pretty, and she would never forget this. He was TOTGA. In retrospect, Kate recognised they were too young, too shy and very inexperienced, which is the reason nothing was taken further. He left her town to go east to McGill University in Montreal and soon afterwards his parents moved away. But she never forgot him and would never forget him: he still retained a strange, inexplicable power over her. Many years after last seeing him, she totally illegally accessed the police computer and found out he was living in Toronto, working for a large bank. Then, when in Toronto on a course, she made a special trip to see his house — a crazy thing to do ten years since she last spoke to him, having no idea why she went, but this was what infatuation and first loves did to you. To this day, Kate wistfully told them, she still dreams of him: not often, maybe once a year, he features in her subconscious. She concluded that you never really get over TOTGA, and continue to think of them and what could have happened if life had taken a different direction.

Jo knowingly smiled and told the group of a similar experience with Keld, from Denmark, whom she met during the first few weeks of her undergraduate degree. They went out 'as friends' on a couple of occasions, and on the second of these outings, as they said goodbye, he held her hand saying he could not wait for the third time they would be together. For the next few weeks, she searched the campus for him but never saw him again. She later learned he had been taken ill with an air clot on the brain and quickly returned to Denmark for medical treatment. A few weeks afterwards she received a letter from him, in which he said he had never known such chemistry with anyone else and hoped they could build on this. The letter contained a poem written for her — the only man who had ever written her poetry. The poem ended, 'When mountains crumble to the sea, there will always be you for me.' This was her first 'love letter', which she still had, although it was falling apart, having been read and reread many times. They corresponded for a couple of years and eventually the letters dried up, but she still has a photograph of a 24-year-old blond-haired man, dressed in military uniform, about to embark on national service, and still remembered his birthday each year — 28th April. Jo confirmed she occasionally thinks of him, and of what could have happened if he had not been taken ill. In her hormonal darkest times, or at three a.m., when she had trouble sleeping, she tried to imagine what he was doing, whether he was married, whether he had children, and wondered if he ever thought of her. 'He is my "Brad" experience,' she concluded. 'The One That Got Away.' There was no formal goodbye, everything was left unfinished, and when that occurred, the ties did not die. Often, it was only one half of the connection who felt this way, but you never knew for certain.

Daphne sighed, adding regrettably she did not have 'TOTGA' story similar to the others, but felt she is playing the recipient role with Igor. She knew he was completely besotted with her, and even through their time apart, when he was in Sochi and she in Vancouver, when she was trying to forget him, he was thinking of her hourly. His commitment was absolute: she could never imagine a time he would not love her. She reiterated what Kate and Jo had already said — everyone had someone in their life from their past who, for some reason, had and continued to have a profound inexplicable influence; who, despite decades and relocations and marriages to others, and children, they still (often guiltily) thought of, even if they had not encountered that person for decades, and would probably never see them again. It did not have to be a former boyfriend or girlfriend, and frequently it was not. Former lovers leave for a reason: TOTGA individuals had an unspecified magic and a persona which, for some reason, was not explored to the full in the past, and it was for that reason they continued to exert such an inexplicable influence years after the original encounter. What could have been... Andrea was not alone: the only difference was that she revisited her TOTGA and had time to discover the faults.

The eight-day holiday passed quickly and as they said goodbye at Narita Airport, all had tears in their eyes and started to discuss their seventieth-birthday celebration, and where the occasion would be celebrated. Daphne announced that as they were not getting any younger, these meetings needed to be every five years, not every ten years, and the next one would be her treat. She took control, proposing she rent a house — maybe in Hawaii, maybe California — overlooking the ocean, hopefully with a pool, where they could relax, drink wine, cook designer meals, tell stories, invent lies, reminisce, compare wrinkles, grey hairs and flabby skin, stay up late and get up later. They all agreed this would be perfect and would await Daphne's formal invitation. No one thought the event would not happen — why would it not? After all, they each felt the same as they did, aged twenty. With unbridled optimism, goodbyes were said, and Jo walked away from her friends to board her flight to London. The others, holding each other's hands, watched her disappear into a sea of travellers,

On the 28th of November 2019, Andrea turned sixty. Peter arranged a small dinner party to mark the occasion and invited Daphne and Kate, Amy and her boyfriend, Curt. Peter cooked roast lamb with mint sauce, garlic mashed potatoes, fennel, carrots and broccoli. Amy made the cake and Daphne and Kate brought champagne. Having her family and closest friends in this intimate gathering was, for Andrea, the perfect birthday gift. Peter's attention to detail knew no bounds: there were cloth napkins, candles, fine china and polished cutlery, all beautifully arranged in the tight dining space. At the end of the evening, they each gave Andrea gifts; the most special being from Peter, as he presented her with details of their three-week holiday in Japan, including Air Canada flights, a rail-pass for unlimited train travel and nights in numerous hotels in Tokyo, Kyoto, Osaka and other smaller towns, including Yonago, the community where her grandparents were born. They would be leaving on the 20th of July 2020, prior to the opening ceremonies and return when the Games were over.

Despite his sexual orientation, Andrea had consistently held a deep affection for Peter, only recently coming to fully appreciate the extent of this, realising it had increased significantly since commencing her affair with Brad. Initially, she thought she would leave Peter, but now was sure she would not. Their relationship was unconventional, but significantly better than many of those of her friends and colleagues. Peter had never physically assaulted her, nor been mentally cruel, petty or vindictive. He always did his share of domestic chores and was supportive of her work, her ambitions, her interests and her friends. He was funny, interesting and entertaining, and in his own way, she knew he loved and appreciated her. They were best friends, and this birthday gift was perfect for one best friend to give another. If she had any nagging doubts over terminating her relationship with Brad, these were completely laid to rest during this sixtieth-birthday celebration.

Andrea agreed to spend another weekend with Brad before the end of 2019 but, following her time with her girlfriends and Peter's birthday gift, found herself making excuses to delay this. As the weeks approached the Christmas period, she knew Brad would have more commitments in the hardware store, so it was easy to postpone the meeting, arguing that the new year would be better, when there would be more time. Of course, she also knew she was delaying the inevitable, but hoped the lack of phone calls and absence of contact would lead him to suspect what was happening. Unfortunately, this did not happen and when they spoke, he enthused over the planned lifetime together she had promised in the past.

She spoke to him on Christmas Day and New Year's Day, feeling it would be strange not to, explaining there were severe staff shortages, and a lot of extra work at the hospital, including weekends, so it would be very difficult for them to meet until the beginning of February. It became easy to lie. Recognising in the last three months she had been happier not having him in her life, and with the support of her girlfriends, her resolve to terminate the link was unshakeable.

He arrived at Vancouver Airport one Friday evening early in February 2020. Andrea had been feeling tired and ill for a couple of days, a state she attributed to the heavy workload she endured for the last couple of weeks, but knew she could not cancel the weekend, which had been delayed for months. Besides, this was to be the weekend when everything would change. She needed closure.

Feeling hot and feverish, with an annoying dry cough no amount of antibiotics seemed to cure, she met Brad in the domestic arrivals hall, not far from where they first saw each other twenty years ago: their first connection creating so much happiness and joy, yet today's in stark contrast, coming with so much sorrow. Brad normally booked a functional hotel a short shuttle-bus ride from the airport, but on this occasion, he decided to splurge and reserve a room at the Fairmont.

This four-star establishment was at the airport itself, complete with designer restaurants and chic bars frequented by suited businessmen. It was, he explained, to be his Christmas present to Andrea, adding that all he wanted to do was be locked in a lavish room with a large bed and room service, and be with her intensely and intimately for two days. Andrea swallowed hard. Breaking up was clearly not going to be as easy as her girlfriends suggested.

They walked, hand-in-hand, past the various airline gates, to the hotel's entrance and booked in. She felt nervous, hot and dizzy, explaining this to Brad. He quickly brushed it off, saying she would feel better after some sex, wine and food (in that order), kissed the top of her hair, and told her she smelt of poor quality, cheap soap. Exhausted, she tried to explain that working in hospitals made you smell that way. Uninterested in the explanation, he quipped that the hotel's shower and soap would deal with the odour.

This comment she could not take. The flippant retort and lack of compassion for her weak, feverish and apparently smelly body was the final straw. As they approached the allocated bedroom door, she quickly blurted out she could not be with him any more, would not enter the bedroom and needed to end the relationship. Between coughing bouts, with sweat covering her forehead, she spoke the words needed to terminate the relationship in an assured, confident way, surprising both of them, never having spoken to him in this manner before; never having been so sure of herself in anything. Maybe the last time — maybe the only time — she demonstrated such certainty was when leaving her hometown upon learning he was to marry someone else. He opened the bedroom door, looking more annoyed than upset, saying they needed to discuss everything inside, and not create a scene in the corridor of a designer hotel where other guests could hear. Andrea knew that if she entered the room, he would be in control, and her fragile resolve lost. She also knew she was not at all well, and all she desired now was to go to bed and snuggle beneath a duvet with copious amounts of pain medication.

'I'm sorry — really sorry — but my mind is made up. This is over,' she said, as she walked back towards the elevator, praying he would not follow her. Waiting for the elevator to arrive, she glanced down the corridor to the room he had reserved. He had entered. This was, indeed, the end.

Andrea caught a taxi home. She had not expected to find Peter there as he was currently juggling numerous jobs, including working for the University of British Columbia as an on-call physiotherapist in their Sports Medicine Clinic, employed in a couple of private, long-term care homes, as well as addressing the demands of a few private clients. In all the time they had been together he always balanced a patchwork of positions, seeming to thrive on variety, broad age ranges and the diversity of his patients. He was in the kitchen, kneading bread, as she entered. Dropping her jacket on the floor, she explained she was not feeling well, immediately searching the kitchen drawer for suitable pain killers.

'I'm not feeling great, either,' he said, adding he planned to treat his ailments by lying on the sofa with a glass of red wine and Netflix for the next few hours. Andrea took the medication and headed upstairs, feeling awful, yet pleased the encounter she had been dreading was over, but also a little regretful that the relationship with the individual who figured so prominently throughout her life was over. All those years of obsessing, of wondering where he was, what he was doing, of finding him again, the elation and excitement and — at one stage — deep, true love; then the slow, gradual, careful courtship and reconnection, all to end in disappointment. The man you hoped you had, at long last, found proving to be not the one you sought. Who was it who said, 'You can never go back'?

She expected that Brad would try to contact her and the hotel corridor goodbye would not be the final act, and there would be a tacit understanding while they would never be lovers or special friends, they would keep in touch. But as the month of February ended, she realised he was not going to search her out, and if she wanted to retain a link, it would be for her to initiate. She was, however, aware of the clichéd comment that everyone guilty of initiating a break-up employs — 'Lets remain friends' — which the wounded party knows is merely a technique to enable the instigator to feel better. Agonising over this, Andrea questioned whether, if she did make the first move, Brad would read too much into it, believing she had changed her mind. Or would he, like her, be satisfied and thankful of a distant 'staying in touch'? If things remained as they were, she had again lost an influential part of her teenage, developing years. She had lost the ability to reminisce about events shared with only one other person; that person being unique and special. She had lost contact with her first love. One Friday evening in March, when Peter was out, and after a couple of glasses of wine she needed for courage, she phoned the hardware store and asked to speak to him.

The young girl answering the phone sounded flustered, saying she would get the manager. The male, clear voice Andrea was connected to immediately enquired if she was a good friend of Brad. Andrea explained she was an old school friend, who maintained intermittent contact. The manager cleared his throat, and giving a statement he had clearly delivered before, coldly told her Brad had passed away a few days ago. Without prompting, he went on to explain, with no emotion in his voice, that it was a shock, but a few weekends ago Brad had gone to Vancouver to visit friends and upon returning, he had fallen ill. Initially, everyone thought it was just a bad dose of the flu but later, when it was too late, it became apparent that he had contracted the coronavirus. He died from the symptoms. The manager added that he was the first victim in their small, tight-knit community.

Andrea thanked him and put the phone down, shaking. Undoubtedly, Brad had been infected through his contact with her. She and Peter had been infected, through their work, before the extent of the Covid 19 pandemic had been fully realised, but neither suffered severely: they just carried the virus. Both felt tired, hot, run down and feverish for about a week, tested positive, and then self-isolated for two weeks: both fully recovered. Brad, who she now remembered had respiratory issues in his teenage years, was not that fortunate. She had unknowingly infected her lover and killed him.

She could not share this knowledge with anyone except, of course, Jo, Kate and Daphne. How linked their lives were. Four women, who initially, when they met in 1984 at the University of British Columbia, had little in common, developed a bond few others experience, becoming the closest of friends. One's partner's life was terminated, at his insistence, as the others looked on; another partner's life was ended by his wife, but seen as an accident; another partner's life was taken by a lover; and now her first boyfriend's life had been snatched by a virus received from her husband and transmitted through her.

Peter should never know the facts. She suspected he had contracted the virus through his work at numerous care homes and passed it to her. As March

2020 dawned, the world started to close down as the realisation of the extent of the global pandemic became undeniable, dominating everyone's lives. The television news showed lockdowns initially in areas of China, then spreading to the western democracies of Italy, Spain, France and Great Britain, then to New Zealand, Australia, India, South Africa, Brazil and finally, the USA. Ice hockey arenas were converted to morgues and convention centres to hospitals; mass graves were dug in New York and social isolation became the rallying cry. The demand for surgical masks, hand sanitisers and respirators sored as the world applauded the healthcare workers and others on the front line. And each day, the grim figures showing the numbers infected and those who had died were published. By early May, Andrea managed to stop blaming herself for Brad's death. Thousands of people died and were going to die by the end of the pandemic. By that time, it was probable that everyone would know someone who would be a victim. Brad's death was one of the early ones, when travel and social isolating guidelines were not fully in place. Better to consider it as an accident. Better not to think of it at all and try to move on.

March 2020 also saw the cancellation, or postponement, of many sports events as the pandemic strengthened its hold across the globe. The NBA in the USA; all soccer fixtures in Europe; Formula One motor racing; and the 2020 Tokyo Summer Olympics, which were postponed until 2021. Never before had the

Olympic Games been postponed, although they had been cancelled during the First and Second World Wars. Peter was deeply disappointed, although fully appreciating and understanding the decision. While Andrea's work at the hospital became more intense and stressful, his work dried up, so he started volunteering his time within the health sector, finding positions through his contacts. During extended periods in the house, he worked on his culinary skills. Andrea returned home exhausted, but in the knowledge that dinner would be superb. Many couples found stresses in their relationship during this period of lockdown, but Andrea and Peter experienced no such tensions and instead, seemed to grow closer.

In April 2020, the Canadian Olympic Organising Committee informed Peter that his talents would not be needed in Tokyo in 2020 but hoped he would be able to take an active role in 2021, in whatever manner the Games were to take place. Japan had invested considerable sums of money to secure the Games and, as a nation, was immensely proud to be hosting them. Tokyo's Metropolitan Government set aside US$3.67 billion to fund the Games: when they were postponed, almost five million tickets had been sold. Over eleven thousand athletes from two hundred and six countries were expected to compete in forty-two competition venues. A 'New Launch Task Force' was quickly announced to oversee the postponement. Everyone involved was disappointed, but those in Japan were determined they would take place, in some form, a year later. At this time, there was considerable discussion over whether there would be any Games at all in 2021, but Peter wanted to be true to his word, and his promise to Andrea, telling her that whether or not the Games took place, they would be in Japan in July 2021 and celebrate her sixtieth birthday as planned, albeit belatedly.

With the Games postponed and the world closed to international travel, Peter spent a day in forced isolation, re-booking flights and accommodation in the reluctant acceptance that Andrea's sixtieth-birthday gift and his involvement in the Tokyo 2020 Olympics were to be delayed a year. They would still be known as the 2020 Summer Olympics, although taking place in 2021.

Peter and Andrea boarded the Air Canada flight from Vancouver to Tokyo on Tuesday July 20th, 2021, a year after they expected to. Tokyo's main airport — known as Narita International Airport — is located sixty kilometres east of the city. The airport staff had gone to great lengths to ensure the many international visitors were greeted warmly. After landing, Andrea and Peter walked for what seemed like miles, past huge LCD panels featuring scenes from the country of cherry-blossom trees, smiling petite women in traditional dress, temples, exotic birds, mountains and waterfalls, creating a distracting view for their tired bodies, following the ten-hour flight. These images were stunning but could not compensate for the long journey needed to reach the centre of Tokyo, and their hotel.

At first, the bus journey away from the airport progressed quickly, speeding through countryside and a rural vista, but they quickly slowed as it entered the rubric of roads characterising the outskirts of the capital. The travel agent had suggested a medium-sized, 'Western style' hotel, close to the main transportation system, subway system and good access routes, with a comprehensive buffet breakfast catering for every taste. It was not cheap, but nothing in this once-in-a-life-time trip was. Four hours after their flight landed, they checked into the contemporary hotel, somewhat difficult to find, hidden between restaurants, offices, and shops in a bustling street. It was six p.m. The hotel staff spoke perfect English and gave them two room keys as they realised, with considerable relief, that they had at last reached their destination. Taking the elevator to the sixth floor, they entered the compact, neat, twin-bedded room. The street below was busy, but the room silent. Ignoring hunger pangs, they went straight to bed.

On Friday 24th July 2021, the day of the planned opening Olympic ceremonies, Peter woke early, excited at being in a new city, with a childlike anticipation of what the day would deliver, but still suffering a little from jet lag and a body clock well out of sync. He looked across at Andrea, who was still fast asleep. 7.23 a.m., the clock radio stated. Quietly getting up, he took his clothes from the previous evening and entered the bathroom to silently get dressed, thinking he would go for a walk for an hour to the park and temple they had visited the day before, and then return for breakfast, by which time she would be awake.

The black-suited reception staff bowed as he left the hotel and he bowed back, already adoring this established custom, reminiscent of times gone by, when the world was slower, traditional and more formal. The day was already hot and sticky. Dark clouds were forming, threatening the onset of heavy rain. Having no rain jacket or umbrella, he hoped the deluge was not imminent. After a brief walk, he entered the one-hundred-and-seventy-acre park surrounding the famous Meiji-jingu shrine. Three buses of tourists were disgorging, and he quickened his pace to avoid the slow-moving throng clogging the pavements. A guidebook informed him that Tokyo had thirty-five temples, but he knew this temple, with its central location and wonderful forest, to be the most popular. Despite the hour, it was extremely busy, and not for the first time did he question whether this sticky, expensive, sixtieth-birthday gift was a good idea. Large gravel roads led to the entrance of the park and following the stream of visitors, he headed to the large temple, surrounded by souvenir shops and cafes, enjoyed the previous day with Andrea. He smiled to himself as he remembered it, thinking to himself how they were getting on very well, seeming to have arrived at a different plateau in their marriage. Their bond was growing as they aged together. Reservations he may have had over the years over their relationship, and whether it would endure, were abating. Life was good. These shops were to be his end point, after which he would return to the hotel, and Andrea would be up and they could eat. He was very hungry.

Before arriving at his intended destination, unannounced, intermittent heavy drops of rain disrupted his thoughts, and he quickly decided he needed to return to avoid the downpour. These intended actions came too late. By the time he returned to the park's entrance, his white shirt was soaked and transparent, clinging unbecomingly to his skin, revealing a torso that had seen better days. He squelched along in wet sandals, cursing himself for not having the foresight to pick up one of the hotel's complementary umbrellas, clearly displayed in the lobby. After another twenty minutes, he sheepishly entered the hotel, praying the reception would be too preoccupied to notice his arrival, and the puddles of water he was about to deposit on the shining, black-tiled, polished floor. They were not. All smiled and bowed.

Starting to unbutton his shirt in the elevator, he was keen to quickly get out of his drenched attire. Opening the bedroom door, he found the room silent, still in complete darkness. She must have been really tired, he thought, a little annoyed he would need to wake her and wait longer for the food his stomach noisily craved.

Entering the bathroom to remove his wet clothes, Peter took the white cotton dressing gown, supplied by the hotel, from the bathroom door, and without drying his body, put it on. Walking over to the bedroom windows, he pulled the curtains ajar to reveal a vista of high-rises and closely packed buildings. The clock brightly announced it was 9.08 a.m. He turned to look at her: she was on her back, wearing a light-blue, long nightshirt that Amy had bought her, with the image of a black bear, paws raised, yawning, and the words: 'I can't bear mornings.' She looked odd — white, and completely still. He stared at her, then sat on the edge of her bed. Something was not right. He nervously stretched out his hand to touch her arm. She was cold. He tried to find her pulse: there was none. Then he bent to listen for a heartbeat. Nothing. His stomach churned; through hunger or shock, he did not know. He continued to stare, with no emotion, as the slow realisation that Andrea was dead took hold.

He continued to sit on the bed, one hundred and one thoughts peppering his brain. How could she be dead, he reasoned. There had been no illness when they went to bed last night. No fever. Yesterday, they walked for over five hours, and although both admitted their legs ached, this was only to be blamed on the fact that the action was not one undertaken regularly. They ate at the hotel, no dubious street food passing their lips: sushi and miso soup and a salad with noodles. There was no history of illness in the family. She was not taking any medication. People aged sixty do not just suddenly die for no reason. It did not make sense.

As if with an uncanny premonition, he recognised these moments alone with her body, in this Japanese hotel bedroom, as unique. In an irrational way, he started to anticipate what was about to happen. Currently, he was the only one aware of what had occurred. In a few minutes, he would need to necessitate a sequence of events which would take on a life of their own; events he would have no control over. He would miss taking the famous bullet trains, exploring Kyoto, Hiroshima, hiking on Mount Fuji. He would need to tell Amy, who adored her mother; and Daphne, Jo and Kate, all who loved her dearly; her work colleagues, her friends. And all would look at him sympathetically and offer condolences. He would need to learn how to pay the household bills online, find out the day that garbage was collected, look for her bank and social-media passwords.

He got up from the bed and wondered what to wear; whether to tidy away the pile of wet clothes lying on the bathroom floor before going to inform the nice, bowing, black-suited women in the reception, who could not make eye contact. What a way to disrupt their day. Should he shower? It was already 9.23 a.m. There may not be an opportunity later, but if he did, and the police questioned the reception staff as to the time between his return and informing them of Andrea's death, it may seem macabre if there had been a large elapse of time.

It was strange to think of this statement: 'Andrea is dead.' 'My wife is dead.' 'I think my wife has died.' It was similar to visiting a foreign country, and having only elementary knowledge of the language and yet wanting to order a beer and be understood, so like repeating the required perfect phrase — 'une bière, s'il vous plaît', 'una cerveza, por favor' — he practiced informing a Japanese stranger that his wife had died. No matter how he tried, he could not conjugate the words needed. As these thoughts ran through his mind, it suddenly occurred to him that in concentrating on the logistics, he had failed to feel any actual emotion. Tears, sadness, loss had not been addressed. So far, only the practicalities had been considered.

He did not love her in the conventional husband and wife way: he had never loved her that way, but he did love her. Theirs had been a partnership — two people who met when young and who found it easier to encounter the world as a couple than as single beings. Two people pretending, wanting to share a home, to fulfil convention, to honour their Catholic faith and meet the expectations of their families, but in reality, fulfilling a pretence. This was certainly true in the early days and was equally true now. He recalled what his mother told him when his father, whom his sisters never liked, passed away. She told him it was going to be difficult for them to grieve, as they would experience little sadness and feel guilty at not being upset, contrasting with the pain he had. At that time, he considered his siblings and mother heartless and cruel, but now, as Andrea's lifeless body lay a few feet away from him, he could identify. He felt little emotion, knowing this would come. His mind was currently preoccupied with the practicalities, not his own loss or grief.

Shaking himself out of introspection, he told himself to get dressed. He must start to process the situation. He looked at her again, still peaceful. Clad in a crumpled large T-shirt with a yawning bear, he tried to pull it down to cover more of her thighs, attempting to dignify the corpse, with little success. He then went to the wardrobe to retrieve dark shorts, a white linen short-sleeved shirt and light blue canvas shoes. The shoes did not match his attire, but as his sandals were soaked, they provided the only option. At 9.38 a.m., he left bedroom number 605 to report the death of his wife to the bowing hotel-reception staff.

During the brief elevator ride, he decided it preferable to ask to speak to the manager, rather than ruin the day of his younger colleagues. Three large television screens were switched on without sound, causing a distraction for Peter to focus on. The manager arrived quickly, a clone of his younger staff, with black suit and bows. Peter took him aside and spoke the now well-rehearsed words, 'I think my wife is dead.' The manager showed total composure, as if this occurrence was a daily event, and suggested they return to the room, taking the key from Peter as they entered the elevator.

They rode in silence. Upon reaching the room, the manager requested Peter wait outside, which he did — but not for long. Within moments, the manager emerged, suggesting they return to his office. Again, there was no conversation. Despite speaking fluent English, this man obviously decided it was not the time to engage in small talk with a Canadian man who had experienced a considerable shock. In passing the reception, he quickly conveyed to his staff something which Peter easily understood to mean, 'Do not disturb me for a couple of hours as there has been a crisis.' Peter noticed the three silent televisions were championing more joyous events: a game show, a soap opera, wrestling. He wondered why they were there.

Upon entering his small, well organised and neat office, the manager introduced himself as Mr Sato, stating the obvious by telling Peter these were unusual circumstances, and at first appearance it would seem his wife had died, and that being the case, he would need to contact the local police service. There then followed the audible, embarrassing sound of Peter's stomach churning. He had not eaten since the previous evening, and quickly explained this. Mr. Sato bowed again, and said he quite understood, suggesting he would arrange for a plate of pastries and fruit to be delivered to his office with either tea or coffee. Peter opted for coffee, offered thanks and bowed. It was becoming contagious.

Mr Sato then spoke to the police service by telephone and upon terminating the call, stood up and told Peter to remain in his office and the officers would arrive shortly, after which he left but returned quickly with a copy of the Japanese Times. At the same moment, a tray of coffee and pastries were delivered. Mr Sato left, locking the door behind him.

Peter sat alone in the neat, windowless office, wondering how long 'shortly' meant in Japanese police terms. He could hear people in the street outside; trucks reversing, garage doors opening, voices shouting, day-to-day commercial business taking place. If he listened hard, he could hear televisions. Peter had left his phone in the bedroom but felt little inclination to call anyone or access emails or texts. He dreaded starting the chain of events announcing her death. He ate a second pastry and poured himself more coffee. He looked for a clock, but there was not one. He started debating whether to help himself to a third pastry when the door was unlocked and Mr Sato re-entered, with two contrasting police officers. The first officer was a man in his fifties with grey, short hair, wearing a flat 'captain' hat, navy-blue vest with numerous pockets, all containing some item (pepper spray, note book, flash-light), dark pants and light-blue shirt. The second was a much younger, female officer in the same attire, but wearing a baseball-style cap. They bowed and Peter stood up and bowed back. The female officer spoke fluent English, and it soon became apparent that her colleague did not; an issue which provoked some tension between the duo. Clearly, the male officer wanted to take control but was reliant on his younger female colleague. Sparks, all be them subtle, were flying.

The four left the office and took the elevator to the sixth floor. The manager spoke to the male police officer, and the female officer smiled sympathetically at Peter. He attempted to smile back, telling himself he needed to get used to this action, as he would undoubtedly be required to draw upon the response on countless occasions in the near future. Mr Sato entered the room first, as he had the key. The curtains were still half drawn. Peter was immediately aware of a strange smell; maybe his damp clothes, or maybe the smell of a dead body left unattended for hours. He wondered if the others noticed. Both officers moved towards Andrea. The male officer took hold of her wrist, felt for a pulse and then moved to search for a heartbeat. The well-rehearsed words Peter had spoken to Mr Sato needed clarification: he could have been lying. They all spoke quietly amongst themselves and then the female officer turned to Peter, compassion in her eyes. She addressed him in short, precise, well-articulated sentences.

'Mr. Sato has arranged for another room to be made available for you. We must contact a doctor to determine what happened. We will contact the Canadian consulate for you. They will be helpful. They are always very busy. We have to take your passport. We also have to take your phone. We will return them to you soon. We are all very sorry.' With that, she nervously looked at her boss, who nodded, although obviously understood nothing. Peter's shoulders started to shake and silently, he started to cry. The two Japanese men looked embarrassed, but the younger officer took his arm and led him from the bedroom to the corridor and away from Andrea's body. That was the last time he saw her.

The man from the Canadian Embassy arrived a couple of hours later. Peter had been shown to another hotel bedroom where he could shower. Another tray of food — tea and sushi — had been delivered. Peter sat on the bed, trying to watch the television, but did not find an English language channel, so gave up. It felt a little odd to be left alone. He took the telephone pad and pen and attempted to make a list of things he needed to do, people he should tell, actions required, in an attempt to feel he was doing something. It was futile.

Carl Manfold was a man in his late twenties who clearly had some experience with the sudden deaths of Canadians abroad. He was obviously junior enough to be easily dispensable, as all other embassy staff, he jealously stated, were busy with an international diplomatic banquet. Carl was, however, of sufficient rank to deal with the situation. He wore black trousers, sandals and a short-sleeved cotton shirt with a couple of maple-leaf pins in the lapel. Peter speculated whether he had been told to wear these, or if it was by choice. He had perfect teeth and thinning blond hair, which would be gone completely in five years. A large man-sack was slung over his shoulder, which he seemed unacquainted with as he kept altering its position. He sniffed a lot, which annoyed Peter.

Upon entering the bedroom, Carl was already flustered. The small room was not conducive to two western men who had never met before, speaking of a tragic unexplained death. Carl knew enough to suggest they go to a bar, so he could explain what would be happening next, and where the environment was less cramped. To Peter's relief, there was no attempt at small talk as they left the room and entered the elevator. Carl was forgiven for his sniffling.

The bar was practically empty. The big television screens replicated those in the lobby, showing images but thankfully, Peter thought, displaying no sound. Both men ordered Japanese beers and Carl tried his best to show compassion. It became apparent that he was a man for whom any emotion was difficult to convey, making him ideal civil-service material, Peter thought. After the required, 'I'm so sorry for your loss. It must have been quite a shock,' Carl explained that Andrea's body had now been removed. Thankfully realising he was not dealing with a highly emotional, distraught spouse, he went on to state there would be an autopsy to determine the cause of death and to rule out any foul play. Carl was careful not to imply that Peter could be involved in any way. He expected this would only take a matter of days, but Peter would not be able to leave Tokyo until the results were known. The police would be keeping his passport and phone, but Peter could contact friends and relatives through the Embassy. Carl was at pains to stress that the Embassy was his friend in a foreign land, and if there was anything he needed, he had only to ask. Peter tried to smile, but smiles were difficult at this time. He just ended up looking like someone who did not get the joke when everyone else did, smiling to feel part of the group. Peter began to see a lot of himself in Carl.

For the Canadian official, it was all very practical, well-rehearsed, organised and clean. He had dealt with many similar situations during his three-year posting in Japan. The only difference between this death and thousands of others that occur when people are travelling in foreign lands, was that this one occurred to Peter and was personal to him. Unbeknown to Carl, it would also irretrievably influence the lives of three women who were the victim's closest friends, ensuring these lives would never be the same again. But this was not his concern. Carl just needed to complete the paperwork, ensure the boxes had been ticked, all aspects dealt with, the body returned to Canada, the Japanese police happy, so he could move on and hopefully be invited to the much-anticipated Italian wine-tasting reception next week, without any similar distractions.

His conversation with Carl concluded, Peter was shown to the new room allocated for the remainder of his stay. He sat on the bed, legs outstretched, glass of whisky in hand. He had made no attempt to contact anyone, shed no more tears, nor felt any strong emotion. He just felt numb, deciding intoxication and sleep was the best way to end this day. At nine p.m., there was a loud knock on his door. Struggling to wake, and unsure of his surroundings, it took a few seconds before he remembered. Carl was at the door, seeking permission to enter.

Andrea had died of a pulmonary embolism: a severe blood clot in the lungs which starts in the legs, travels to the lungs and can prevent oxygen getting to the heart, which can cause heart attacks and death. Known as the 'Silent Killer', this fate often befalls people who have taken long flights, or who are inactive over long periods of time. There are frequently symptoms prior to the event, such as tiredness, shortness of breath and aching legs. Andrea displayed none, or if she did, these were not conveyed to Peter. It was totally unpredictable. The coroner quickly delivered a verdict of death by natural causes. Three days after finding her lifeless body, Peter's passport and telephone were returned and he was free to leave. Carl arranged for the body to be returned to Canada. Peter saw nothing of Tokyo or Japan, having little desire to do so alone, sheading no more tears until he returned to Canada.

A month after the death, a memorial service took place in Vancouver at the Catholic church Andrea infrequently attended. Over one hundred friends and colleagues were there; a testimony to how popular she was. Jo had flown over from England to pay her respects and be with Kate and Daphne. They, of course, all felt the loss very deeply. Peter asked if any of them wanted to speak at the service, but they declined, each realising the raw emotions and grief felt would prevent any attempt at delivering a coherent address. Peter gave a lovely, sensitive eulogy on behalf of Amy and himself, leaving no one in any doubt that their loss was significant as they started to build a life without her.

After the church service was over, Peter and Amy invited close friends to return to their house, but none of the three women felt able to. Kate suggested they toast Andrea's life by visiting a small bar she knew, not far from the church, adding it would have been the send-off Andrea would have wanted from her three closest friends. All agreed.

The bar clearly did not greet many customers at two p.m. on a weekday afternoon. They settled into a booth and ordered a bottle of Pino Gris — Andrea's preferred wine — but no food. No one had any appetite. Despite having been informed of Andrea's death over a month ago, the three women had been unable to accept it. They never anticipated a time when there would not be the four of them. In all their experiences together, they never, even hypothetically, discussed their deaths, nor imagined who would be first, nor how or when they would die. Over the years, all had lost partners, parents, acquaintances, colleagues, key individuals in their lives, and dealt with these deaths, but not thought that this could occur to their best friend — to one of the special group.

'It is just impossible to think of her gone,' Daphne said, taking large gulps of wine. Both Kate and Jo knew Daphne shared the most with Andrea, and vice versa, and would be feeling the most pain.

'We have to move on,' added Kate. 'It is difficult. As a group, we will never be the same again, Andrea will always be part of us — it's like someone cut off our right arm. She will never be forgotten, but it is important to focus on the good times; the priceless, unique memories she left us with.'

Kate went on to reflect that, since learning of Andrea's death, she had spent more time thinking about all of them, and what their friendship meant to her. She realised the bond they had had outlived all their marriages. The secrets told, the experiences shared, and the years they built together provided testament that this group could never be replaced. Although having siblings, she confessed to feeling closer to her three girlfriends than her blood relatives. She shared DNA with others, but this did not signify she was closer to them. She was not. Daphne, Jo and Andrea were her real sisters. While society could offer clichés, such as 'blood is thicker than water', and marriage is 'til death do us part,' for her, it was friendship — and specifically their friendship — which mattered the most. Within this group she could share every feeling, every emotion, every vulnerability, every stupid idea, or intimate reflection. When good things happened in her life, she sought to tell them first. When bad things happened, or there was devastating news, she wanted to run to them, be comforted by them, talk everything out with them; having, of course, done so. She never felt this relationship was not reciprocal: it was almost frightening to think how close they were. They all supported each other, shared secrets, had fun, their bond unique. Andrea's sudden, untimely death was devastating for them, but she was so thankful they had met and been close for so long. It was undoubtedly the most important thing in her life. This friendship had been essential to her health and happiness over the years. Kate stopped, looking a little embarrassed, then apologised for her lengthy outburst.

'You always were the thinker and analyser,' said Jo, between sobs. 'I think you have just managed to articulate all my thoughts and feelings, with the exception of one.'

Jo added that since Andrea's death, she was now preoccupied by mortality, and more specifically their deaths, wondering who would be next and who would be left when the others had gone. 'Can you imagine being the last one alive, not having the support we have all depended on over the years, being alone without your best friends?' No one spoke as the three women reflected on the tragic scenario Jo outlined. Kate, still dabbing her eyes with sodden tissues, suggested this was a not a subject to be addressed now, when they were all raw, reminding them they were still young. This was not the time to introduce morbid thoughts.

The three women raised their glasses, toasted Andrea and then sat silently, waiting for someone to introduce a suitable subject.

'Our next birthday meeting will be so different,' Daphne mused. 'Remember, I suggested meeting in Hawaii? I don't think I want to do that now.' She added that it would seem strange as it was originally discussed with Andrea, and she would be absent. Andrea was part of the original idea. The others agreed, then Jo said she had just read an article about the next Summer Olympics, which was to be in Paris in 2024 — the year they would all turn sixty-five — and as their lives had been tied to the Games, they should meet in Paris. Fate happening again. They raised their glasses toasting Paris 2024. Daphne paid for the wine and they left the bar, 'United by Emotion.'

Epilogue
One World, One Dream
Beijing, Winter Olympics 2022

Jo woke following a disturbed night's sleep, in the large, anonymous hotel bedroom that had been her home for the last seven days. The perpetual hum of the heating system was the only audible sound. She looked up at the large, black, gold and red floral print above her king size bed, then turned to focus on the desk in the corner of the room, and the debris deposited on it. Four Olympic mascot toys – black and white smiling bears, clad in white bodysuits – lay next to a large coffee mug with the motto; "One World, One Dream" scripted in red and blue. She yawned and closed her eyes, reflecting on the deeply concerning conversation she had had last night with a beautiful, intelligent, engaging women of a similar age, who could have been her sister, friend, or lover, except she lived on another continent and was of a totally different culture.

Chen Wang was the sales manager for Reliable Plastic Products Inc, a Chinese company who supplied large quantities of plastic sealant application tools, sealant guns and packaging tubes to Holden Sealants. Holden was one of their largest, and most reliable, long standing customers. As the 2022 winter Olympics was to be held in Beijing, Jo was invited to attend as their guest. Consequently, Chen had been tasked to ensure no stone was left unturned to ensure this highly respected customer experienced an unforgettable time and, of course, continued to order their products. The original invitation had been sent to Bernard Trim, the CEO of Holden, but he quickly decided not to attend, having no interest in receiving such attention from this supplier. While he acknowledged the important place such invitations had in conducting and cementing business relationships, he also recognised it was something he was more than happy to delegate. In his experience, many of these prestigious social invitations went on too long, involved individuals with whom he had little in common (and who clearly had an alternative agenda), would likely never meet again, and who he seldom actually liked. The invite to Beijing was to take place over many days, in a foreign land, a long way from his North Yorkshire comfort zone. It would involve unfamiliar cuisines and require a considerable time commitment away from his English home. He was more than happy to assign another. Consequently, it was Jo who found herself waking up in the plush bedroom of a five-star luxury hotel in Beijing.

Jo and Chen shared the same job description within their respective companies, and while during the first couple of days they spent together they retained a detached, somewhat formal contact, over the course of time, as they got to know each other, this had abated. They got on well, liked each other and had developed a good rapport. Jo suspected Chen was gay but knew not to ask.

This chilly February morning was to be Jo's last day in Beijing. In a few hours Chen would arrive to take her to the airport, their paths never to pass again. Jo got out of bed, picked up one of the mascot bears and started to twist it in her hands, replaying over and over in her head the confession Chen had made to her the previous evening.

The two women had returned to Jo's hotel for dinner, choosing this establishment as it had a large spacious restaurant with well spaced tables, and an extensive Western and Asian menu, in contrast to many other restaurants in the city, which were crowded with Olympic enthusiasts. The air was also considerably cleaner. At one point in the conversation Jo casually spoke of Chen's career development, comparing it to her own, whereupon Chen's expression changed, and she looked close to tears. She confessed that in two days she would be leaving the company she loved to stay at home to care for her mother-in-law. She explained that entertaining Jo for the last seven days had been her last task for the employer she had been with for over twenty-five years.

Jo could immediately tell this turn of events was not welcome. As delicately as she was able, she sought an explanation of why this decision had been made.

Chen then unfolded a heartbreaking story involving a husband, who she clearly had little affection for, his two sisters and their incontinent, frail, eighty-six-year-old mother, who spoke a different dialect, and suffered with dementia. As the only male sibling, Chen's husband had been tasked with looking after his parent, as neither sister wanted, nor felt able to.

Two weeks ago the mother, now unable to live alone, had moved into Chen's small two bedroomed apartment. Chen went on to describe the layers of plastic which now covered all her furniture and flooring, the perpetual smell of urine as the woman refused to wear disposable underwear and consequently needed to be changed and cleaned regularly. The old women spent her days seated in front of the television screen, chain smoking. She also had to be spoon fed. As Chen only spoke Mandarin and English they could not communicate.

Jo asked about Chen's husband and learned he was spending longer periods out of the house, and when Jo asked why a care home could not be found it became apparent that the family did not approve of this option. Chen added that in this culture it was her responsibility to follow the desires of her husband and not to question him. The three siblings had reluctantly agreed to take turns to care for their mother until Chen finished work. In two days, she would leave the employment she loved and start a new life as a full-time care giver to her mother-in-law.

Jo went into the bathroom, turned on the shower and sat on the toilet studying the numerous adjacent buttons to control its heat, tilt and water flow. Twelve days remained before the closing ceremonies and the end of the Beijing Olympics. Should she truthfully confess to Chen the events and people who had previously controlled and influenced her life? Should she outline the extent of pain and misery she had felt and hidden for decades and how this was eventually addressed during the London Olympics ten years ago? Should she confess to the unbelievable happiness which can be derived when you have the courage to take control of your life and make radical choices, in the full knowledge that these choices may cause physical and mental harm to some but will benefit others far more? At this point she wondered if there were a Kate, Daphne or Andrea in Chen's life, if she had the support and counsel of true female friends she could trust and rely on, who would not judge her and who would be with her no matter what she did or said or thought; but in an instant Jo knew there was not. Chen was completely alone.

Jo exited the bathroom and switched on the television. A panoramic image of the Bird's Nest Stadium filled the screen, followed by footage of spectators arriving and taking their places in the banner filled arena. She muted the sound and started to pack her suitcase, uncertain of what direction the following few hours would take.

Printed in Great Britain
by Amazon